James Rigg

Wild flower lyrics and other poems

James Rigg

Wild flower lyrics and other poems

ISBN/EAN: 9783744722728

Printed in Europe, USA, Canada, Australia, Japan

Cover: Foto ©Andreas Hilbeck / pixelio.de

More available books at **www.hansebooks.com**

Wild Flower Lyrics

And Other Poems

BY

JAMES RIGG

HAIL ! sweet messengers of Heaven !
 Angels of the mystic Light.
God to man hath message given
 In your glorious eyes so bright !
Man adores your silent greeting
While your fairy forms are fleeting
 From the ravished fields and fells,
Where your fearful forms are springing,
And your censers sweet are swinging
 Incense to your chiming bells !

ALEXANDER GARDNER

Publisher to Her Majesty the Queen

PAISLEY; AND PATERNOSTER SQUARE, LONDON

1897

PREFACE.

From boyhood I have been in love with the Wildlings : I rank them among my teachers and preachers. To me, as to thousands, they ever seem to whisper such sweet things, and tell such strange and fairy-like stories of their present and past existence, that they appeal to the highest faculties of our being.

The following pieces, therefore, are, for the most part, the outflowings of my heart to the lovely flowers that adorn our lanes, fields and fells, and that smile upon us and cheer and bless us in our country rambles.

I offer my verses, such as they are, chiefly to the denizens of our big Mammon-worshipping cities, in the hope that they may help to lighten the burden of "Sordid Wealth" that weighs so heavily on tens of thousands. If they should be the means of leading one here and there with a lighter heart and keener perception into Nature's fair domain—there to gather imperishable treasures from the lovely blossoms that kiss the clear brooks and mountain wells, or that smile up to us from our country lanes and bypaths—I shall have done my little to check the Nature-forgetting tendencies of city life.

"Natural Selection" being now generally admitted to be the chief factor in the life history of Flowers, I have, in many of my pieces, referred to this great law.

That these "Wild Flower Lyrics" may give profit and pleasure to many, and be an offence to none, is the devout wish of the Author.

18 Wilton Drive,
    Glasgow, *June 1897.*

CONTENTS.

(The figures in brackets indicate the pages where the Flowers, etc., occur incidentally in other poems.)

CONTENTS.

MISCELLANEOUS POEMS.

WILD FLOWER LYRICS.

THE PROGRESS OF QUEEN FLORA, ADORNED BY A HUNDRED WILD FLOWERS.

In dreamland once I Flora saw
  By all her flowers arrayed,
As through the months she lightly trod—
  O'er hill, by brook and glade.
Not Venus—flower of ocean's foam—
  Was half so fair to see :—
The peerless queen without a stain—
  Her looks woke harmony !
First JANUARY, in ermine cloak,
  With crystal spangles dight,
He gave the queen an Ivy crown,
  And her fair shoulders white
He happ'd with tender ferny Moss
  From many a cosy nook,
Or from the rounded boulders warm
  Beside the frozen brook.
Next, FEBRUARY, from her lap
  Of white and grey and green
Brought tiny tufts of Whitlow-grass
  As offering to the queen ;

A

And Hazel Catkins, too, she hung
    About the Ivy crown,
And Willow's silvery studs she sewed
    Upon her Snowdrop gown !
Then MARCH lit all his Crocus lamps,
    And, in the Celandine,—
While rang the chimes of Daffodils—
    He brought her dainty wine.
Then round her brows he deftly set
    The Chickweed's pretty rays ;
And tossed the Wood-Anemone
    All through the warmer days.
Then Tussilago strewed her path—
    With yellow guineas bright—
An offering to the beauteous queen :
    Sloe blossoms gave her light ;
And all about the mountain brooks
    The Golden-Saxifrage
Presented her with brooches rare
    To cheer her pilgrimage !
Ground-Ivy, last, a garland wove,
    With Amethysts begemmed,
And bound it round her beaming brows :
    Her feet a brooklet stemmed
As 'neath soft APRIL showers she passed,
    And Moschatel's wee clocks
Chimed out their fairy peals, beneath
    The Primrose on the rocks.
The Willow's silver turned to gold
    By her fair fingers white,
And Goldilocks in glory shone
    Beneath her glances bright.

Her mantle brushed the new-lit fires
  Of flushed Marsh-Marigold ;
And in her hair shone Stitchwort stars
  Of beauties manifold.
And then I saw queen Flora smile,
  Her eyes grow bright as day,
As canopied with Hawthorn white
  She paced the courts of MAY,
Who robed her in the golden Broom,
  With skirt of Speedwell blue,
Beflounced with fragrant Hyacinth,
  The Cuckoo-flower's pale hue—
Red Campion, Wood-sorrel pale—
  Courting the crystal linn :
While all the air with gladness held
  The dairy smell of Whinn.
The Wallflower nodded from the rock,
  The Maple choired with bees ;
Sweet Myrrh, Woodruff, the Bugle flower,
  Tall Comfrey—yea, all these
The goddess saw, well pleased, I trow ;
  But may I sing how she
With nimble feet, divinely neat,
  Light skimmed the Daisy lea ?—
Till she embraced bright Rose-crowned JUNE
  'Neath Birch trees' leafy showers,
Where Foxgloves tall as sentries stood
  To guard the fragrant bowers.
The Charlock gleamed o'er corny fields,
  And, that gay millionaire
The Dandelion, flung his wealth
  Around her feet so fair !

Here golden King-cups glittering stood ;
   Orchid did purple don ;
Rock-Roses rare, and London Pride,
   In meads the Bogbean shone
Like lamps. There Cranesbills and Monkshood,
   And Gromell brightly blue
Rejoiced ; and o'er the little pools
   The Crowfoot's white flakes flew :
Rich was the goddess fair attired
   As JULY did her greet
With Fleur-de-luce, Forget-me-nots,
   And Violets pure and sweet ;
Convolvulus and Tufted-Vetch
   Round Flora's brows she twined,
And scarlet Poppies, Campion,
   Sea-pinks and Mallows kind :
Rose-bay and Purple Loosestrife tall,
   St. John's Worts, bells of Heath ;
The Lime trees fragrant honey dropped ;
   The Water-lilies' breath
Arose as incense from the lake
   Whose waters, rippling, played
Soft whispering music to the queen.
   Here Flora long had stayed—
But AUGUST gives a welcome, too :—
   Her Bellflowers welcome chime !—
White Clover and the Woodbine blend
   Their smells with purpled Thyme.
The Lady's-mantle by the brook,
   The Corn-flower 'mong the wheat,
The Tansy among ruins old,
   Came forth their queen to greet :—

Gay Hawkweeds, Milkworts, Kidney Vetch,
　　Grass-of-Parnassus star ;
While Ox-eye-Daisy's living suns
　　Blazed out both near and far !
Then mild SEPTEMBER, Heather clad,
　　Her cheeks with Berries dyed,
Lit all her lamps (the scarlet Hyps)—
　　She with the others vied
To please the queen.　A Golden-Rod
　　She gave her ; and her locks
She hung with Hair-bells, azure blue,
　　And Bedstraw from the rocks,
And Eye-bright, too, to bless her eyes ;
　　Then on her bosom white
She placed the fragrant leaves of Mint
　　For Flora's dear delight.
Gay Galeopsis on her dress
　　She pinned ; and round her waist
Ripe clusters hung of Brambles black,
　　And bade the goddess taste !
OCTOBER round her snowy neck
　　Bright Nightshade berries hung,
And Ivy-leaved-Toadflax she wove
　　For Flora's forehead young :
With Gentian blue her robe she trimmed ;
　　And her of storms to tell,
She placed within her lily hand
　　The scarlet Pimpernell :
Then for a crown both rich and rare,
　　Of beauties manifold,
She placed upon the goddess' head
　　The bright Corn-marigold !

NOVEMBER gave her scented sprigs
  Of Spruce and Larch and Pine ;
And in DECEMBER'S gloomy shades
  Some Chickweed stars did shine.
One Daisy, too, the bleak month gave
  To baffle melancholy ;
And e'en I saw fair Flora smile
  When crowned with crimson Holly !
And then the queen of all the flowers
  Passed onward, soft and slow—
Her radiant brows adorned with Pearls
  Of sacred Mistletoe !

HYMN TO THE FLOWERS.

HAIL! sweet messengers of Heaven!
  Angels of the mystic Light.
God to man hath message given
  In your glorious eyes so bright!
Man adores your silent greeting
While your fairy forms are fleeting
  From the ravished fields and fells,
Where your lovely forms are springing,
And your censers sweet are swinging
  Incense to your chiming bells!

God's own pictures—Earth adorning—
  Brightest effluence of His will,
Beauty of creation's morning,
  Beauty of all mystery still.
If th' Unseen Himself declare
In your wondrous forms so fair ;
  Who may once His working trace,
Or may see the unerring hand
That within you Life first fanned,
  Robing you in matchless grace ?

Love doth ever hover round you,
  And his fingers fair, divine,
Have with priceless treasures crowned you,
  That in leaf and petal shine ;
Still the quick-eyed insect telling
Where your honied founts are welling.

Tell us, Nature's jewels bright,
Have ye joy when children's eyes
Gaze into your paradise ?—
    Giving—do ye feel delight ?

Sweetly are your odours stealing
    Through the wooing summer air ;
To man's inner self revealing
    Images of Eden fair :
And your hues so manifold—
Prophetic of the age of gold—
    Strike the adoring inner eye,
Bright revealings of the day
When man quits his house of clay
    For his palace in the sky !

MOSS.

Some of our prettiest and cloth-like mosses are seen at their best in late winter ; on old walls, by the roots of hedges, or in the sounding glens that ring to the snowy torrents, their lovely forms are to be met with—giving man a new pleasure ; and doubtless, what to us is a carpet of soft velvet, to the fairies will appear vast forests of pines.

THOUGH the naked woods in exile moan
　　Beneath grim Winter's sway ;
While his borean blast round the boles is lash'd
　　Till each mourns for the Spring's soft sway :—
Though stripped and chilled all the branches toss,
Yet cosie beneath lies the verdant Moss.

The walls that in Summer wore sere and brown,
　　And ever looked old by the year in prime,
Each donneth in Winter its emerald gown
　　Bejewelled with beads of the silvery rime :
And deep in the dells where the fairies cross
In the moonlight dance, grows the gay green Moss.

Though the flowers be fled, and the earth's fair face
　　Is veiled by the crispy snow ;
Yet Nature is still in her secret mill—
　　For the Moss grows green below ;—
There our darling mother is spinning her floss
　　And weaving a robe of the emerald Moss !

And when sprightly Spring blows his bugle bold
　　Till the world "RESURGUM" rings,
When his bright Daffodils are kissed by the rills
　　And the forest his welcome sings—
As he filleth his cups of the golden gloss,
Then his feet fall soft on the ferny Moss !

"THE BUGLE NOTES OF SPRING."

Now, Winter, on his ice-bound car,
Is rattling north, o'er crag and scar ;
The thrush and blackbird cheery sing—
Blowing the bugle notes of Spring :
    Saying, " Coming ! coming ! coming !
    The Spring is coming, man, to thee ! "

I've heard for many a year, ah me !
Those bugle notes so wild and free ;
And though each year its wrinkle throws,
That music aye the sweeter grows—
    Saying, "Coming ! coming ! coming !
    Perennial youth I bring with me."

The Celandine's bright cup of gold
Is nestling by the brooklet cold ;
The Coltsfoot to the warming days
Is streaming back its yellow rays :
    Saying, " Coming ! coming ! coming !
    Sweet Flora cometh, fair to see."

The Chestnut bursts its shining hoods,
The Poplar scents the leafing woods,
Where, cheerfully, among the boughs,
The birds are warbling tender vows,
    Saying, "Coming ? coming ? coming ?
    And spend the Summer, love, with me ! "

And my dull muse it fain would sing
Of the bonnie bugle notes of spring :—
" O blackbird, in thy ecstasy,
Chant thy loud clarion cheerily !
    While, humming ! humming ! humming !
    The words repeat thy song for me."

TO THE SNOWDROP.

(*Galanthus Nivalis.*)

LONE lady of the leafless woods,
  Pure herald of the Spring,
Thy gauzy skirt soft frilled with green,
  Thy cloak, a seraph's wing !

Sweet, nodding 'mong the dewy moss,
  No sister flower to cheer,
Alone, thou deck'st the silent glade,
  Dear firstling of the year !

Ere Spring hath donned his vernal robe,
  Ere Flora opes her hand,
To waft her incense on the air,
  And paint the ravished land—

Thou wakest from thy wintry sleep,
  Like Hope in deepest gloom,
And tellest me of brighter days,
  Of life beyond the tomb.

Thou image white of Chastity,
  A drop all undefiled,
I gaze upon thee till I seem
  Again a little child !

Too bashful for the pageantry
  Of summer's regal halls,
How modestly thou comest forth
  Ere yet the cuckoo calls.

Yet, wilt not stay, e'en to behold
  The golden daffodils ;
Nor hear the throstle charm the dawn
  And all the woodland rills.

Go, lovely maiden of the dell,
  Thy image shall abide
A thing of hope and sanctity
  Whatever may betide !

TO THE SNOWDROP—(HOPE).

DARLING, that shun'st the glow of Summer's heat,
Here, through the leafless woods, in skirt of green
And robe that dims the snow, thou com'st to greet
The glories of the year that long have been
Imprisoned by stern Winter's ruthless hand !
Thou com'st the first of Flora's lovely band.
I mark thy virgin form in quiet nook—
Sweet emblem of the pure, the true and good :
Thy lovely bell e'en deigneth not to look
Toward the lord of day : and thou'lt not brood
On evils past and gone. Thou point'st to me
A warmer, brighter ray—dear lady of the lea !

ON THE SAME FLOWER.

THERE'S an ancient wood, and I know it well,
Where the meek, meek maid of the mossy dell—
The Snowdrop, robed in the living Light—
(A gleam of hope in the longing night)—
Proclaims anew that the Spring is near
And the flowery pageant of the year.
O, this lady of Light, I call her Hope,
For the gates of Heaven her fingers ope ;
And she bids us bask in its cloudless ray,
With the loved ones lost in our wintry day.

TO THE "NONE-SO-PRETTY," OR LONDON PRIDE.

(Saxifraga Umbrosa.)

IMAGE of sweetness—lovely gem !
A fairy's sceptre's thy starry stem ;
Young Jenny a-tripping the daisied lea,
In innocence and maiden glee ;
Or the witching glance of the dark-eyed Hetty,
Are just like thee, my " *None-so-Pretty.*"

TO THE WHITLOW-GRASS.

(Draba Verna.)

This little messenger of Spring is not a grass at all—it is one of the cruifera. It is found growing on walls and waste places in February and March, and its tiny snowy blossoms, set on stems often no more than an inch high, are sweet, if not gaudy, after Winter's weary reign has come to an end.

O, WHY should I, still singing, pass
Thy elfin form, wee Whitlow-grass !
On farmer's dyke, by crumblin' wa',
Thy tiny blossoms, pale as snaw,
Are aye the first to welcome Spring,
An' wauk my drowsy muse to sing !
Ere Winter ower the Grampians clanks
I see thee crowd the staney banks :
Like white-clad bairns thy floorits play,
Haudin' their wee short holiday.
Beneath the scuddin' sleety skies
Thou blinkest like a sweet surprise,
An' mak'st thy modest curtesie
Ere yet a flower-bell swings the bee ;
Nor shall thy bashful eyes behold
Gay Summer all her charms unfold !—
Thou courtest not Life's looking-glass,
My white-veiled sister—Whitlow-grass.

TO THE COMMON CHICKWEED.

(*Stellaria Minor.*)

Examine this little wayside star, and you may not think I rave of
its sweet, neat, snowy beauty.

DAY-STARNIE o' the poet's e'e,
Thy wee white rays shed joy on me!
By rough roadsides hoo bonnilie
    Thy blossoms blink;
Whane'er thy tender form I see,
    Thou gar'st me think.

When Winter rives the inky lift,
An' bings the banks wi' snawy drift,
'Neath some bit bield thou mak'st a shift
    To gie a glint,
An' bring the Icy King a gift,
    When a' seems tint.

Lang ere the fields are fleck'd wi' kine,
Or Spring hath gloss'd the Celandine,
Or Tussilago opes her mine
    Of treasures bright,
Hoo sweet thy constellations shine
    Sae snawy white.

Let folks e'en ca' thee "Chicken-weed"—
Thy beauty raises sic a breed
O' bonnie thoughts within ma heid
    Pen canna match them;
And gleg e'ed Fancy, famed for speed,
    Can seldom catch them.

Noo, on this bonnie day o' spring,
Thy wee, gay, juicy leaves I'se bring
To Dickie wi' the yellow wing,
    To clear his throat ;
There, on his bauk, he'll thankfu' sing
    A blither note.

TO THE GOAT WILLOW.

(*Salex Caprea.*)

The following lines might apply to nearly the whole family of Willows ; but the above species is exceedingly pretty in the early spring-time.

I.

RICH rover of the water-ways !
Gold garland of young Spring,
As up the hazel'd glen he strays
And makes his clarion ring.

II.

Thy Cathkins, clad in silver, dance
Like snowflakes by the stream ;
Then, quick, ere Summer's flowers advance,
In brightest gold they gleam.

III.

Thy blossoms dust the purpling dawn
Of Hyacinthine glades ;
But ere the Daisy creams the lawn
Their golden splendour fades.

IV.

How sweet thy bending branches twine
A silken soft Boudoir
To shield the polished Celandine
And Anemoné so fair.

V.

Wan Willow by the wimpling burn—
O, joy of Youth and Age—
Invite me still, at Spring's return,
To read fond Nature's page.

TO THE COMMON-GROUNDSEL.

(Senecio Vulgaris.)

This common weed of cultivation, to perpetuate itself, flowers all through the year. It follows in the track of civilisation, and is certainly not beloved by the gardener or husbandman. Nevertheless, an ordinary magnifying glass applied to its head of flowers reveals to the eye a cluster of lilies of wondrous beauty.

My puir wee persecuted cronie,
Sair ca'd and cuffed—ne'er praised by onie—
Let me noo sing thy gowden bonnet—
A bab o' lilies, worth a sonnet !
Wee tawted type o' Labour—haurl'd
Frae birth tae death thro' this cauld warld ;
Whyles rakéd here, and hirsled there,
By some roadside, 'neath hedges bare—
Like some puir poet " crowded out "
Frae ilka journal roun' about,
Waitin' a nod frae men o' letters,
Or maybe bobbin' 'mang his betters,—
Still sighing for some passing bliss,
That, grasping, still he's sure to miss !

By dawner byngs or cottar's midden,
Or, 'mang the gentry's flowers, unbidden,
Thou cock'st thy downy toosie tappy,
Nor ever seem'st tae tak' a nappy
Like brawer flowers that bloom a blink,
Syne cosy 'neath the divots sink—
For, e'en in blusterin' cauld December,
When bairnies gather roun' the fender,

Thy dragled form I often spy
By some auld hoose or grumphy's stye,
Nursing thy weans 'mong sleet an' snaw—
Biding the winter's bitter blaw !

Thou hast an unco facht, my frien'—
A' thro' the year you're somewhaur seen ;
And, maybe, could you tell your life,
'Twad be a tale o' lengthen'd strife
Frae happier days and sunny climes
Down tae the day your poet rhymes.
Darwinians say that in Life's race
You're aiblins shortenin' your pace,
An' tho' aft aided wi' the win'
You're doubtless laggin' far ahin' ;
Yet gif we're bless'd wi' store o' patience,
Baith you an' I shall fill our stations !

DAFFODILS.

SOLOMON, Ophir, splendour, glory—
   These are the Court of the Daffodils
By the silent woods so gray and hoary,
   'Mong the ferny moss by the dripping rills.

Spring with its fluty voice is singing—
   Winter is hastening over the hills—
Lightly the laughing hours are bringing
   Wealth to the home of the Daffodils.

O, Love in each golden Cup doth hide,
   And wine of the soul each chalice fills ;
And the pure in heart alone may bide
   By the hallowed haunts of the Daffodils.

Now, while their golden bells are ringing
   Music that all my being thrills,
Grateful my heart anew is winging
   Thanks for the days of the Daffodils !

TO THE DAFFODIL.

HERALD of the floral year,
Come once more our hearts to cheer,
While Throstles all the woods do trill
O'er thy head bright Daffodil ;

How thy glory fills my heart,
There young fancies keenly dart
While the woods I roam at will,
Courting thee, sweet Daffodil !

Youth perennial comes to me
When thy royal charms I see
In mossy groves beneath the mill,
Gold bespangled Daffodil !

Music of the coming year
Ever in thy bell I hear
Ringing thro' the woodland still,
Fresh, bright, nodding Daffodil !

Now thy brightest gold refined
In dark ringlets I will bind :
Love thy precious cup doth fill—
Lovely, lovely Daffodil !

TO THE COLTS-FOOT OR TUSSILAGO.

(Tussilago Farfara.)

O, TUSSILAGO all the day,
O, Tussilago all the way !—
From bouldered banks and drossy heaps
Thy golden glory upward leaps ;
I need not go to El Dorado—
Thou art my treasure—Tussilago !

On grassless knolls, by paths and streams,
I mark thy ever welcome gleams ;
And feel again a child at play
All through this sweet young April day ;
Tho' gold may woo by false bravado,
Thou ne'er deceivest—Tussilago !

Like Charity in dusky lanes ;
Like Mercy's ever cheering strains,
So opes thy disk of living light
To beat the Poet's fancy bright :
From thy low bed of dross or clay
Thou hast made glad this April day !

TO THE TUSSILAGO (No. 2).

HAIL! lowly flower! The first to cheer
The ransomed earth from Winter's spear,
And lead the van in Flora's year—
        Queen Tussilago!

Dark hid beneath thy bed of clay
Thou did'st prepare each golden ray
To light the poet on his way—
        Dear Tussilago!

And from thy golden treasury
Thou strewest wealth on bank and lea,
And sayest, "It is all for thee,"—
        Loved Tussilago!

Each year I mark thee gladsome gleam
O'er barren spots, by bank and stream
I dream again a childhood's dream—
        Gay Tussilago!

TO THE TUBEROUS MOSCHATELL, OR FAIRY CLOCKS.

(*Adoxa Moschatellina.*)

This tiny green-flowered harbinger of the spring is found about dry banks or under hawthorn hedges. Its blossoms give evidence of a queer evolutionary history—they are all five-petalled, save the terminal one on the spike, which carries but four petals. The flowers also have a faint odour of musk : for what purpose ?

WHEN Spring leads in, wi' beaming e'e,
　　His daffodils and lambs,
I wander forth wi' boundin' step
　　About Gleniffer's dams ;
Or up the Glen, whar burnies sten
　　Aroun' sweet "Tannie's" well,
Wi' rovin' glee I seek for thee—
　　Wee, winsome Moschatell.

Thy bonnie, triple-ternate leaves
　　Lie cowerin' 'mang the cleavers,*
A' nicket fine—a deft design
　　For *leadin'* Paisley weavers :
While roun' your stems, like clustered gems,
　　Your flowret's are a spell—
Like tiny clocks for fairy folks—
　　Wee, cunning Moschatell.

Ye dinna flaunt a gaudy flag,
　　To welcome in the spring ;
But lowly, meek, the shade ye seek,
　　Like poets when they sing ;

* Robin-run-the-hedge.

An' to the ear that's gled to hear,
   Yer message saft ye tell,
That broomy braes an' simmer days
   Are near—wee Moschatell.

An' mony a text ye haun' to me,
   Low, unassuming flower :
Short is your stay aneath the brae,
   An' brief is manhood's power ;
Ere summer's rose its perfume blows,
   Thy musk forsakes the dell ;
Yet I hae joys auld Time ne'er cloys—
   Adieu, wee Moschatell.

TO THE LESSER CELANDINE.

(Ranunculus Ficaria.)

I FEAR to dim thy shining gold
  With my dull, misty measure ;
O ! had I words, I might unfold
  The half thou giv'st of pleasure.

How gay thy polished petals greet
  The King of Days returning,
As round the brooklet's margin sweet
  Thy fairy lamps keep burning.

What purest joy pervadeth me,
  Still gazing on thy shining,
While balsam from the poplar tree
  Might heal the heart's repining.

O, joy ! to see old age caress'd
  By youth's full love so tender,
And know that Earth bears on her breast
  The Celandine's bright splendour.

A tender Father sure doth send
  Sweet tidings by thy face ;
I count thee still a beauteous friend,
  A solace, and a grace.

THE LESSER CELANDINE.

(Ranunculus Ficaria.)

THE Larch her scented tassels gay
Hangs high, and bids us come away ;
A chaplet, love, for you I'll twine,
Set with the Suns of Celandine.

We'll rove among the robing woods,
Beneath the Chesnuts' glossy hoods ;
And deep in dells we'll see them shine—
Th' unspotted Suns of Celandine.

We'll skirt the brook so cool and clear,
The Blackbird's lay our hearts shall cheer ;
For sordid wealth we ne'er shall pine—
We've found the golden Celandine.

With your true love, the streams and flowers,
Content shall halo all my hours ;
Nor shall I count what gain is mine—
For I have found the Celandine !

THE LESSER CELANDINE.

(Ranunculus Ficaria.)

I would ask my readers to look into the cup of this little spring flower, and say whether they ever saw a piece of gold so brightly polished.

THROUGH the glen the Throstle's singing—
The woods are all with wooing ringing;
And the fairies sip new wine
From the golden Celandine!

About the lake, their bright array
Doth gladden all this April day;
O, bright the polished petals shine
Of the Lesser Celandine.

Thy beauty, floweret, ne'er was told—
For who can sing thy burnished gold?
Yet in my heart may I ne'er tine
Thy image, Lesser Celandine!

TO THE WILD ANEMONÉ, OR WIND FLOWER.

(Anemoné Nemorosa.)

In the budding Spring, when the woods all ring
   With the bird's clear minstrelsy,
Then I roam the glade for my own sweet maid
    The fair Anemoné.

When the Celandine in its gold doth shine,
   And the cascade leaps in glee—
By its crystal showers, thro' the noonday hours,
    Nods the fairy Anemoné.

O, Wind-flower sweet, when thy form I greet,
   And thy tender blush I see—
Thou recall'st a grace, and a vanished face,
    My lovely Anemoné !

So I'll fondly press thy morn-tipp'd dress—
   For her image abides in thee—
With thy flowers so fair she adorned her hair ;
    I bless thee—Anemoné.

TO THE SPRING GENTIAN.

(Gentiana Verna.)

Some years ago, while on a pedestrian tour among the Swiss Alps, I first came upon some patches of this incomparably blue flower on the summit of the Gemmi Pass, at an elevation of 8000 feet; and I deemed it a rich recompense for my six hours' climbing amid the majesty of the mountains, to gaze and gaze upon its beauty—rendered all the more striking by its surroundings of ice and snow. It is now a rare flower in Britain; but may be seen in bloom on the Rockery at the east end of the Botanic Gardens, Glasgow. Don't touch, please.

HAIL, living Sapphire! Brightly blow
On Alpland's crown of silvery snow!
In thought I hear, with heart aglow,
   Thy mute Hosanna
Arise, where choiring waters flow,—
   Blue Gentiana!

Far from the languorous rosy vale
Where lovers tell the young-old tale
Thou bloom'st alone, where none assail
   Thy form so tender,
And spreadest to the Alpine gale
   Thy skiey splendour!

When through the deep cerulean blue
The queen of flowers thy petals drew
And gave to Earth a gem like you—
   A heavenly prize—
She strewed thee where thou yet might'st view
   Thy natal skies!

Thy azure beauty well doth pay
My climbing half this summer day ;
I call thee mine ; and well may say
       Thou art a treasure—
A living truth to cheer life's way—
       A lasting pleasure !

TO A PRIMROSE I SAW BLOOM IN
JANUARY.

WITH joy I've wandered in the greening lanes,
To catch a glimpse of thy pure saffron cup,
Sweet Primrose—when the Chestnut's glossy buds
Were fragrant with the coying of the Spring;
And marked thee (with that fondness in my heart
That comes with vernal sweets and fresh delights
Of the dear Springtime) smiling in some nook
Beneath a mossy scar that gently dripp'd
Into thy bosom pure dew's liquid pearls;
And then I knew the beauty of the year
Again was nigh—fast following thy soft steps
Through glen and brake, and o'er the upland lea,
While dappled skies, the Celandine's bright cup,
And music showering through the larky air,
Proclaimed that Nature once again was young!
How hath grim Winter thus deceived thee, child!
For, ere the Willow had refined its gold,
Or yet the Moschatell hath set its clocks,
I mark thee, maiden of the moss-clad dell,
A shivering suppliant for his scanty beams!—
His looks betrayed but to allure thee hence!
But yesterday I saw thee bide his blasts—
To-day thy sweetness feeds his hungry frost!

TO THE PRIMROSE.

(*Primula Vulgaris.*)

SOFT, saffron beauty of the Spring,
  Meek maiden of the glen,
I'd travel half an April day
In hopes to meet thee by the way,
  Or in cool, mossy den.

Mine is a pilgrimage of love
  To meet thee once again;
Dear, after Winter's icy storm,
To see thee raise thy moonlit form,
  To bless the eyes of men.

Thy silken form by rippling rill,
  Or jewelled cascade bright,
I saw with glee when yet a boy;
I mark thee now with deeper joy
  In manhood's clearer light.

Methinks thou art surpassing fair,
  When, high above the stream,
Thou bloom'st secure upon the rock,
Nor heedest how the torrents mock—
  A maiden in a dream.

The lily and the rose shall reign
  When Summer's sun is high;
But thy sweet breath holds all the glade,
Nor can I meet a fairer maid,
  While Spring doth rule the sky.

TO THE SHEPHERD'S PURSE.

(Capsella Bursa Pastora.)

WHAT a queer little chap thou art, sure, my Capsella ;
Why, the fairies must deem thee a rich little fellow.
Eight Months of the Twelve thou dost hire as thy
    nurses,*
And well each is paid, by a largess of purses.

Thou hast no pretensions to sweetness or beauty—
But just all the year thou art doing thy duty.
Thy pinnatified leaves, tho', a bodice might make
For Titania so fair as she frisks thro' the brake !

I would stare till my eyes started out of their sockets,
Were I sure I should know *how* you fashion your
    pockets,
Or *how* you can pack 'neath each green tiny fold
Your round living treasures—more precious than
    gold ! †

I note you hang out your wee purses so queer,
And the winds waft your money abroad far and near :
And like words of the meek that keep cheering life's
    way,
I mark thee, with joy, wherever I stray.

---

* It flourishes nearly the whole year round, and is found everywhere.
† Its seeds.

TO THE COMMON CHICKWEED.

(Stellaria Media.)

In order to keep up in the race for life, this plant is obliged to flower all the year round, and is everywhere showing off its pretty little stars.

THY magnitude, 'mong Flora's stars,
    I scarcely may define ;
But cloud nor cold thy image mars—
    I ever see thee shine.

By stubble field or roughest path
    Thy pretty rays blink clear,
Like one that sure a mission hath
    To preach through all the year !

So, kindly words and simple ways
    Are faith enough for me ;
Why long for singing sunny days ?
    The Year makes Harmony !

TO THE COMMON ASH, IN SPRING.

(Fraxinus Excelsior.)

THE LAST TO DON AND THE FIRST TO DOFF.

" The tardy ash, that wilt not robe herself
  When all the woods are green."—*Tennyson.*

WHY stand you a-gazing all the day,
Thy antlers * spread like a stag at bay ?
Dost thou hear how the woods and the welkin ring
To the clarion clear of the bright-eyed Spring ?
He is marching 'mong daisies and daffodils,
And the smell of his garments his temple fills,
The willows their silver have changed to gold,
And the throstle his love hath ten times told;
And the yellow guineas the coltsfoot strew
O'er the bouldered banks—they are not for you.
O, hard is thy heart ! Awake ! come away !—
Thou art missing the spring-time holiday.
O, "Coming, coming," I hear thee whine ;
But thy face is red with the purple wine.†
" With rimy Winter I've banqueted long,
And his nectar hath made my heart feel strong ;
I have no mind for your minstrelsy,
Nor the celandine's gay pageantry ;
I'm a practical tree, with a hard behest,
And to prince and peasant I give my best ;
For I give myself, when my limbs grow old,
To fashion their implements manifold;

---

* Look at the angles of its branches—very like the stag's horns.
† The Ash buds are a wine colour.

Hammer and axe, and axletree,
And chariot wheels—they are all of me.
And, poet, I would that thy fleeting song
Were sturdy as I, enduring, strong—
Not the ephem'ral thing of an hour,
Like a fading rose in a lady's bower.
Tho' I tarry so late in my winter hall,
And hear not the blackbird's early call :
For the sons of men in their dinful strife
I've been storing a treasure for their sweet life.
Then why should the bard of the flowers complain
If I come not forth at his warm refrain ?
Tho' I muse awhile ere I go to print,
Yet I give you a book with a purpose in't."

THE WALL MOSS.

FAIR Flora hath fled to the sunny south,
 But hath left us a robe of green ;
It is hung by the halls of the waterfalls,
 And the haunts of the fairy queen.

'Tis Winter, and all the trees are bare,
 Yet the orchard wall is gay
In its mantle of moss of the virgin green,
 And rich as a lawn in May.

Like a fairy forest of fragrant pines,
 On a fairy mountain high,
Is the 'witching moss on the orchard wall
 To Imagination's eye.

How tender the moss on the orchard wall:
 How charming its vernal green
In the scanty rays of the wintry days,
 When a floweret ne'er is seen.

So I love the moss on the old gray wall,
 For it knoweth nought of art,
And it makes me glad when the days are sad,
 And its beauty fills my heart.

TO THE WATER-CRESS.

Nasturtium Officinale.) .

ON SEEING IT EXPOSED FOR SALE ON A HAWKER'S BARROW IN GLASGOW.

While residing at Barrhead a favourite walk of mine of a Sunday morning (before breakfasting and going to church) was to the famous spring well at the foot of the Neilston Pad, where the salad of the verses grew fresh and plentiful. Three miles either way, with a bit of buttered oat-cake, a handful of cresses, a drink from the fountain, and a half hour for meditation amid the lark's song, the bleating of lambs, and the wild bravoora of the curlew—was a rare preparation for a feast of fat things —temporal and spiritual.

I HA'E an itching to express
My thanks to thee—wee Watercress.
Thou bear'st nae winsome flowers an' braw ;
But sweet wee starnies, white as snaw,
Reflected in the siller stream
Whaur aft, in Spring, I long to dream !
Thou'rt no a plant to tak' the e'e
Or wauken up a poet's glee :
Sae, plain this truth to you I'll blab—
Your strong appeal is to the gab !

Amid the city's sins an' coom
I ken that Winter's surly gloom
Is northward gane, when on some barrow
The sicht o' thee my saul does harrow
For that I canna see thy hame
Whaur burnies toddle—an' the flame
O' gowden Whin blooms lichts the braes
Whaur mony a snawy lambkin plays !

Thy image mony a memory wakes
O' Sawbath mornings—crumpy cakes *
Weel buttered o'er—my rung in haun—
A three mile spin without a staun—
A clear wee rill, whaur thine ain sel'
Grew fresh an' green, aneath the Fell—
A feastin' fine ; while ower us rang
The Lavrock's lay, loud, clear, an' lang ;
An' roun' us Snipes an' Plovers wheeled,
An' Peesweeps screamed o'er ilka field.
An' then, wi' sober thochts an' wise,
My mind aft shot far yont the skies
Tae yon blest river, crystal clear,
Whaur trees bloom bonnie a' the year.

Then frae that kirk aneath the hill—
My heart weel cleaned o' monie an ill—
I joined in Zion's solemn Psalm
Wi' fewer cares, an' felt a calm
Steal ower me at the hour o' prayer—
Since I had quaffed the mornin' air.

Sic hallowed mem'ries, I confess,
Thou help'st to wauken—Water-Cress !

---

* Oat cakes.

TO THE CROCUS.

I am not sure of a plural for this joy of our lawns ; so "crocus"
had better stand for both the singular and the plural.

In galaxies, all up and down
The greening lawn—like girls from town,
In purple, orange, or snowy gown—
    I hail thee, lovely Crocus !

And now that weary Winter's o'er,
Like fairy lanterns round my door
Your lights make glad my eyes once more,
    And warm my heart, bright Crocus.

Among your living, golden lamps
The bitter March wind heedless tramps ;
Yet mighty Sol with beauty stamps
    Your glowing fires, bright Crocus.

But this glad day the winds are still,
And snowy lambs are on the hill,
And raptured bees do sip at will
    Your honied wells, sweet Crocus.

With keener joys my eyes behold
This lowly flower its form unfold ;
Nor would I weigh 'gainst mines of gold
    The treasures of the Crocus.

TO THE DAISY.

(Bellis Perennis.)

WITH fresh delights of years gone bye,
  O'er Nature's carpet now I stray ;
Beside thee, Daisy, now I lie,
  And feel once more a child at play.

Thy ruby lips the morning sun
  Did gently kiss with soft caresses ;
'Tis burning noon, thy love he's won,—
  He's playing 'mong thy golden tresses !

Thy pretty form now robes the field
  In gold and snow, thou " Eye of Day "—
(Thy ancient name) and thou dost yield
  Rare numbers to the Poet's lay.

Thy " milky-way " of spotless suns
  Harmonious shine—no din or strife—
And, as in me, in thee there runs
  Th' unending mystery of Life :—

So that thy disk and dazzling rays
  In silence still proclaim a story
More wondrous than the sun's, whose blaze
  Floods earth and air with light and glory.

Yet, " Beautiful for ever," thou
  Art still the pearl of every lea ;
And wilt be decking childhood's brow
  When he who sings sleeps silently.

LINES ON THE DAISY.

THE pearls of ocean let others prize;
But a richer gem, 'neath the dappled skies,
Is the Daisy, dight in its sunny dyes—
    The Pearl o' the Lea!

TO THE DANDELION.

(Taraxicum Dans Leonis.)

Hail! Cheerer of the rough roadside!
The Springtime's joy, the Summer's pride;
Thou never dost thy treasures hide
     By brake or sedge;
But strew'st thy wealth both far and wide
     By path and hedge!

Thou art a joy to weary eyes—
Thy virtues are a priceless prize—
Thou mak'st the poor dyspeptic rise
     To ruddy health,
Aud wander forth 'neath azure skies
     To bless thy wealth.

The charm of children on the green—
The crown and garland of their queen—
While on its crutch old age will lean
     To catch thy rays,
That waken many a playful scene
     Of childhood's days!

Let misers count their glittering hoard,
Let gamblers court the guinead board;—
A keener joy thy charms afford,
     All undefiled,
When deep thou strik'st thy tender chord
     In Nature's child!

LINES

ON THE DANDELION, IN ITS PAPUS STAGE.

It is instructive and pleasing to watch how the Dandelion makes provision for keeping alive its name. When the flowers appear above the earth on the stalk, they lie until fully matured close on their natal bed, then rising erect the Involucre or curtain opens their full-fledged beauty to the sun. They soon lay a banquet of honey for the insects, and in a few days the curtain closes around them once more, and again they lie down close to earth—out of harm of wind and rain, until their future offspring (the seeds) are matured, when on their parent stem they again exalt themselves, and open to the warm caresses of the sun, each furnished with a papus or balloon. On their airy, fairy parachutes they are borne away by the passing breeze, to germinate over the fields or by the rough waysides.

THE POET TO THE DANDELION.

My dear Millionaire, have you left yourself bare
   Of the gold which you drew from the sun ?
You that ne'er had a fellow in turn-out of yellow—
   Is all your gay pageantry done ?

Once in splendour you shone like a king on a throne,
   With your banquet aye spread for the bee !
Yet, my eyes are enriched, and my senses bewitched—
   For your children about you I see !

In close order they stand to await your command,
   'Neath their parachutes pretty and clean ;
Now your blessing impart ere they're sundered apart,
   Like their sire, golden harvests to glean.

But whither away must your children to-day ?—
    Must they visit the shades of Lunardi—
In those airy balloons—to the zephyr's soft tunes—
    Don't you think they are rather foolhardy ?

But, look ! while I stare, they are off through the air
    With never a cheer nor a rattle—
Like a fleet in full sail : how they bend to the gale,
    And with each windy wave how they battle !

THE DANDELION TO THE POET.

I have spent all my gold on my heirs manifold,
    And in silk I have sent them away,
That each may aspire like its dying old sire
    To make wealth out of each sunny ray.

Through the fierce Winter wild, when I yet was a child,
    I was reared by the stoney wayside ;
Till the Spring's sunny gleams brought me wealth in
        their beams,
    Then I rode in my beauty with pride !

Oft the bairnies' bright eyes did my splendour surprise,
    And thine own I did often decoy,
Till your heart sung a song to the rainbow-winged
        throng
    At my tables all feasting with joy !

But my night draweth nigh, and with never a sigh,
    I return to my Mother's embrace :
Having spoken my page on Earth's wonderful stage,
    I to Youth and fresh Beauty give place !

ENVOY.

There's a sermon in power cometh up from this flower,
    O, ye selfish ones, lay't well to heart :—
That when sloweth your pace, and endeth Life's race,
    There are others going in at the start.

So, from Love's golden mint, let us give, without stint,
    Kindly words and good cheer to our neighbour,
That Earth may be bless'd with the loveliest and best—
    Yea ! for all human Good let us labour !

SONG—THE WHINNY KNOWE.

*(To John H. Turner, Esq. of Parkhouse, Barrhead,
I gratefully inscribe these lines.)*

O, THE Broom blooms bonnie on the brae,
  An' the Hawthorn creams the vale ;
The Violet and mountain Thyme
  Waft incense on the gale :
But dearer far is the gowden lowe
An' the dairy breath o' the Whinny Knowe !

O, June shakes siller o'er the Birk—
  Draps hinnie frae the Plane—
Whaur the bees a' hum in a holy hymn
  I' their green an' leafy fane :
But my heart grows warm at the gowden lowe
An' the dear delights o' the Whinny Knowe !

O, the crystal burnie streaks the glen,
  Whaur the birdies sing a' day ;
But my een drink lang o' the gowden Whin
  As I sit on the " Trystin' Brae,"
Whaur a vision comes o' a langsyne vow :—
O, the memories dear o' the Whinny Knowe !

TO THE COMMON WHIN.

(*Ulex Europæus.*)

Thou vegetable Porcupine—
    Grim tyrant o' the fields an' fells—
Can ony bard to thee incline,
    Thou source o' aiths, an' groans, an' yells ?
He's plainly mused aneath the min,
That daurs to sing thee—surly Whin.

Yet, minstrels rant o' castles steep,
    An' sturdy men that held them lang ;
Thou art a fortress an' a keep—
    An' surely worthy o' a sang—
Come, jag me weel till I begin
To sing thy micht, ma' sworded Whin.

Thou ance did don a mantle saft
    As onie Broom ; till strife o' years—
Fell *self-protection*—drave thee daft,
    An' turned thy bonnie leaves tae spears ;
Till, noo, Defence aft mak's thee win
Thy Waterloos—heroic Whin !

What clouds o' curses ower thee hing
    Frae farmers, herds, an' shepherds dour ;
Yet, monie a hunted tail an' wing
    Ha'e sheltered 'neath thy bristled tower ;
An' weasles, rodents, reynards rin
Aneath thy shelterin' wa's, ma' Whin.

The wee white fuds * that dot the braes,
   An' nibble 'mong the clover sweet,
Nae fear to waur their furry claes
   Ahint thy bay'nets rin fu' fleet
Whene'er they hear the rifle's din—
Thou art a stronghold, sturdy Whin.

Tak' that in praise o' thy guid mail;
   Noo, let me chant thy gowden bonnet!
'Mang a' things bonnie could I wale
   A theme for an immortal sonnet;
Nae laurels could I ever win,
Sae braw's thy croon, gay Yellow Whin.

It glads ma heart tae wander free
   In early Spring, the flowers tae greet;
An' mang them a' thysel' tae see,
   An' snuff thy dairy breath sae sweet.
Lang may thy lowe licht up the linn—
The warl aye needs a sturdy Whin.

---

* Rabbits.

SPRING-TIME FEELINGS.

WHO hath not felt that inward stirring joy—
    Perhaps not joy—that happy pleasing sense
That comes with vernal bloom and doth decoy
    The longing spirit into thoughts intense.

With mind renewed, I mark the drowsy buds
    Lift up their eyes, when Winter's night is past ;
Or watch adown the hills the foaming floods,
    Or listen to the music of the blast !

TO THE LARCH TREE.

(Abies Larix).

LIKE an emerald set on the breathing breast
  Of the forest, that robes for May—
How thy lightsome verdure my eyes hath bless'd
  In my rambles this April day !—
Let me sing of thee where thy boughs soft arch
O'er the Primrose dainty—my lovely Larch !

By the solemn shade of the sable Pine
  Thou tossest thy tasselled arms,
While thy Rubies rare in the sunlight shine,
  And thy beauty the woodland charms,
And gladness circles thy fragrant air
As love doth girdle a maiden fair !

ENVOI.

When Death, like a Winter, doth leave us bleak,
  And our joys have all ta'en wing,
May a tender friend to our sorrow speak
  Like the Larch to the woods in Spring,
And tell us that summer days are nigh,
When the birds shall sing 'neath a cloudless sky !

TO THE IVY.

(*Hedera Helix.*)

OLD antiquary ! loth to leave
  The crumbling halls of story ;
Like bodied memory, clinging still
  To haunts of legends hoary.

'Mong scenes where love and music reigned,
  Or Freedom called on Duty,
Thou veilest thy immortal limbs
  With fadeless locks of beauty.

I know thou lov'st the singing glen,
  The honeysuckle wooing,
The citron primrose at thy feet,
  Above, the cushat cooing !

But over storied battlements
  In silent power thou ridest ;
And o'er the dust of slumbering kings
  Thy sceptre green abidest.

The raving storm that rifts the oak
  Ne'er scathes thy snaky limbs ;
While 'mong thy leaves the zephyrs sing
  A century of hymns.

Nor scorching suns nor winter's blasts
  Can mar thy ancient splendour ;
And 'neath thy glossy leaves, the birds
  Rear safe their broods so tender.

For them, mayhap, thou hang'st on high*
   Thy berries, black as night,
That each by each, through wondrous Life,
   May keep the balance right.

Dear Ivy ! type of friendship true !
   When Flora's crown doth fade,
Thy rustling band of sober green
   Adorns the queenly maid.

---

* The ivy hangs its berries on the uppermost branches for the birds who in return for this kindness sow far and near the undigested seeds.

THE GROUND-IVY.

(Nepeta Glechoma.)

THERE is a flower that lowly creeps,
And, clad in purple petals, peeps
From 'neath the hedge that skirts a road
Which oft my willing feet have trod :—
Ground-Ivy is its English name ;
And oft, methinks, this flower might shame
Ambitious man.   For, would you view
Its loveliness, it says to you
" Stoop down, adore, and, wiser, see
What beauty clothes Humility."

TO THE SAME FLOWER.

WHY need I wish for sunset skies
To please me with some new surprise ?
Here, 'neath the Hawthorn, bending low
Its angel wings of fragrant snow,
Thy gay imperial purple shines
With rarer charms than India's mines.
Of thee a garland, fragrant, rare,
I'll weave among my true love's hair ;
But, chiefly, when I think of thee,
I learn to love Humility.

TO THE GREATER STITCH-WORT.

(*Stellaria Holstea.*)

BESIDE the Lychnis, robed imperial—
Beneath the lark's loud psalm, aerial—
This noonday lane thou mak'st siderial,
 Bewitching flower !
On thy frail stem, thy form ethereal
 Dost charm this hour.

O that my song were as replete
With beauty as thy petals sweet !
How you and I should lowly greet
 The ear of Praise !
And 'mid earth's plaudits—ever fleet—
 Adorn our days.

TO THE ANNUAL POA GRASS.

(*Poa Annua.*)

This low-spreading grass is found everywhere, and flowers all the
year round ; and it is perhaps the most plentiful plant on our planet.

I SEE the children blithely trip,
And all thy blades with jewels drip:
Across the village green I pass
Where'er I spy thee—tiny grass.

There maids and matrons, with delight,
Oft happed thee up with linen white ;
And yet the more thy carpet's trod
The richer grows thy vernal sod !

With you the Daisy oft I meet—
Thy blades soft-bending at her feet ;
Far fairer looks her crown, I ween,
Enthroned upon thy virgin green.

Thy little tufts of tender spears
Ne'er rusty grow with circling years :
When Winter's snows are o'er thee spread
Thou poppest up thy pearly head.

Yea, like the Anglo-Saxon race,
In every land we see thy face :
Nor would a poet deem it droll
Should Nansen tread thee at the Pole !

No spot for thee is deemed too scant
Whereon a colony to plant : .
My heart to you with fondness clings—
Wee prototype of common things !

SONG OF THE FLOWER-HUNTERS—FOR JUNE.

WITH flowers of the fairest, the gayest, the rarest,
  The hours are arrayed by our dear lady June ;
Then let us away : thro' the glen let us stray,
  Where the deep torrents bass to the Throstle's wild
    tune.

Come away ! come away ! 'Tis a flower-hunter's day,
  We shall climb by the roots of the rock-rifting trees ;
We shall leap the bold stream, where the rare flowerets
    gleam,
  And list to the psalm and the hymn of the bees.

O the scent of the Pines, it is richer than vines
  By the rush of the Rhone or the azure Moselle ;
And the maiden-blushed Rose around us still blows,
  An odour far sweeter than poets can tell.

We will tread the Thymed sward where the Foxgloves
    keep guard,
  Like a troop of Queen Flora's high cap'd grenadiers ;
And, when weary, recline where a thousand stars shine
  And the Orchid its gay purple standard uprears.

Where the Moonwort is peeping, the Club Moss is
    creeping
  'Neath the bleating of snipe and the lapwing's loud
    scream,
And where Violets are nodding, still upwards we're
    plodding—
  Our love is the zephyr, our drink the pure stream.

By nooks that are barest we'll search for the rarest,
   Like truths that lie hid 'mong the peaks of old lore,
But we'll deem it a scandal to once play the vandal,
   And think there are others come here to explore.

'Neath the twitter of swallows, we'll cull the Musk
    Mallows
On banks where the deft Tormentilla lies spread,
And the Grass of Parnassus—we ne'er let it pass us—
   Tho' the bee she deceives with a semblance of bread.*

By the soft mossy bed hang the strawberries red,
   So luscious and ripe by the clear, crystal rill;
And the blaeberries, witching—our senses enriching—
   Inviting our fingers to pluck while we will.

Then homeward we're wending, with joys unending,
   With free bounding step, and cheeks like the rose,
And the vasculum's treasure shall still give us pleasure,
   Until in pure slumber our eyelids shall close.

---

* This pretty flower has a false nectary.

TO THE HEMLOCK PLANT.

(*Conium Maculatum.*)

Hemlock is a deadly poison; and is easily recognised among the Umbelliferous family to which it belongs by the dark blood-like splashes along its stems.

THE Nettle's stings, the Rose's spines,
    The Thistle's cruel spears,
May pain us for a few brief hours,
    And draw, from childhood, tears :
But yet the Rose glad recompense
    Gives back in odour sweet,
And e'en the Thistle waves her plumes
    Our wandering eyes to greet :
But thou, dread Hemlock, hast no charm—
    Giv'st no surcease to pain,
But ever on thy countenance
    Thou bear'st the mark of Cain !
The silent herds that crop the sward
    Know well thy noxious breath ;
And Man, the lord, in thee beholds
    But animated Death !

Beneath thy gloomy brows I see
    The blood still on thy face ;
Nor can the dews of summer ere
    Those gory marks efface !

'Tis well thou bear'st thy dread intent
    Upon thy looks alway :
Perhaps kind Nature so stepped in
    To rob thee of thy prey !

On Earth's fair picture thou mak'st up
   The dark background—that so
We may admire the lovely forms
   That on her canvas glow :
Thus Virtue wore no witchery
   Were Vice not ever near :
Who deck'd the Primrose, made thee too,
   That Man may *love* and *fear*.

THE HUNT FOR THE STAGHORN CLUB-MOSS.

IT is fruity September, bee-hung is the Heather,
The mornin' is dewy, presaging guid weather;
Noo, oor hunt for the Horn in plain Prose I shall tell—
An' the Poetry, fegs, ye maun fill in yersel'.
Sae we're aff for the Ben whaur the Club-mosses grow
'Mang the scars on his face 'neath his bald windy pow.
Feint a rifle or bullet sal waukin oor morn,
Yet ere Sol gangs tae rest we maun bring hame a horn
O' the queer Lycopod. Noo we're scourin' the glen
Whaur the Rowans hang red an' the clear waters sten
Till they linger in linns, in blue crystal repose,
Saft curtain'd wi' ferns: whaur the strawberry grows
An' the Rasp tempts oor fingers wi' sweet juicy blabs
Tae moisten wi' nectar oor gye drouthy gabs!
Hoo the bee-swingin' Heather be-pollens oor breeks
An' the breeze gars the roses rebloom on oor cheeks;
An' the Bog-myrtle's incense perfumes a' the air,
While the Humble-bees hum like a meeting in prayer.
In the saft mossy dens the Cranberry we pou,
Syne we keek thro' the lens at the spangled sun-dew
Wi' her witchin' tiara o' di'monds sae clear—
Invitin' the doom'd thochtless midge tae its bier.
O, the Grass of Parnassus blinks white in the nook,
Like a snawy-skinned nymph that's gaun in for a dook
In the bonnie wee burnie that ever doth sing
Far sweeter, I trow, than my muse on the wing!

Aye upwards we climb, whaur a bush never nods,
We've the tap in oor e'e—an' we mak' oor ain roads,
When—behold! as we pant 'mong the Alpine-flower'd
    stanes,
Here's oor dear Mither's gift tae her three faithfu'
    weans—
Here's the Staghorn sae green spread fu' bonnie to see,
Sewed as firm to the grun as the roots o' a tree;
Ilka steek we snap canny, then the velvetty treasure
We coil roun' oor hats; syne we mount up wi' pleasure
Towards the bald summit. Nae bluid we hae shed
Except whaur we trod on a Crawberry bed.
Wi' oor een fu' o' Bens an' the far sleepin' sea,
We. returned to oor hame 'neath its *vine and fig tree,
Whaur the Yucca Gloriosa dangles high its big bells
An' the robin wi' joy his lowin' breast swells.

---

* Mr. David Davidson, whose guest we were at Garelochhead, has
an aged fig tree in front of his house, loaded with delicious ripe fruit,
and close to it a vine—also bearing in the open air. People have come
from far and near to see his Yucca in bloom—a charming sight.

TO THE GRASS OF PARNASSUS.

(Parnasia Palustris.)

IF on Parnassus dreamy steeps
   The poet breathes celestial air—
As o'er his fancy fitful sweeps
   . Ten thousand images most fair :
Could he to mortals bear below
Aught fairer than thy purpled snow ?

And yet thy beauty's reared by stealth !
   The wooing insects still do chide
Thy mocking show of seeming wealth,
   And find thy feast is *Barmecide.**
Thy charms proclaim a proverb old—
All things that glitter are not gold.

---

* Evolutionists will know the allusion to this pretty flower's *false* nectary.

E

A CHAPTER ON EVOLUTION—THE PANSY'S EYE.

ONE day my boy asked me why
The Pansy hath a yellow eye.
I said I'd try and make it plain
In verse, for *his* and others' gain.

So, first, you know as well as I
The Pansy feels, but can't descry ;
It can't behold its beauteous self,
Altho' admired by maid and elf.

So, what we name a thing of sight,
That gives to you and me delight,
Is just a bower of ecstasie—
A golden gateway for the bee.

She walks across the velvet floor,
And knows right well where lies the store
Of priceless honey ; and in state
She enters by her palace gate—

Prouder than England's vestal Queen,
When o'er the cloak she stepped so clean,
So that's the chief of reasons why
The Pansy hath a yellow eye.

Of *Complementary* shades you've heard ?
To these the Pansy pays regard :
Purple and yellow best combine—
The one doth make the other shine.

More courtly-like the petals seem
When *that* gold eye doth on them beam ;
And it in turn looks brighter too
When robed all day in purple hue.

But all this gaudy show, you see,
Is built—a palace for the bee ;
And she with little din or strife
Weaves thro' the years the Pansy's life.

If Earth's gay insect tribes should die—
No Pansies—like Aurora's sky—
Should greet our gaze ; no beauteous flowers
Should dress the Summer's sunny hours.

TO THE HOP PLANT.

(*Humulus Lupulus.*)

It is the strobiles or catkins of the hop that give the bitter,
appetising property to beer; and who shall say but that England's
success in arms is largely due to her moderate use of the mild
beverage? It is a curious coincidence that the hop leaf very much
resembles that of the vine.

ALL hail ! thou mimic of the vine ;
Long may the muses with thee twine—
Thou that giv'st smack to England's wine,
  The nut-brown ale ;
That mak'st the cot and hall combine
  In friendship hale.

When bearded barley yields his soul
To Britons in the brimming bowl,
Thou, that wast reared around the pole,
  Adjur'st his ghost,
And layest 'neath thy keen control
  Old England's roast.

Tho' Whisky oft remorseless bites,
Yet thou and Malt are cheery sprites
That urge the mind to dear delights
  That seldom cloy,
And wing the Muse for random flights
  Of rural joy.

Tho' Nature stern doth recompense us,
In thee she kindly comes to fence us,
From pangs her broken laws dispense us—
  And early bier,
And hang'st aloft to swell each census,
  Thy strobiles sear.

Let southern bards bluff Bacchus crown,
And fair in song the vine begown ;
Britannia sings her rich Beer brown,
  And, proud, can ope
The story of her fair renown,
  Enwreathed with Hop(e).

TO THE WILD CARROT.

(Daucus Carota.)

This plant belongs to the Umbelliferous order. The florets are very small, but in the umbel they are exceedingly pretty; and, viewed from the under side, form a brooch of Nature's filigree work. In the centre of nearly all the umbels is seen a specialised flower, larger than the normal ones, and varying in colour from pale rose to deep violet or carnation. In the following lines I only theorise as to the *why* the plant has taken to this specialisation. When the petals are spent, and the flowers fertilized, the umbel closes up into the form of a chaffinch's nest.

THE starnie man, wi' queer equations,
May deave us 'bout his constellations,
As, happy, thro' dread space he gropes,
Wi' his big een ca'd telescopes;
But rarer joys this day are mine
To see thy nebulæ a' shine
Wi' steady licht, about the bay,
Wi' yellowing Corn an' Clover gay!

The starry suns, that ever pace
That endless race-course folks ca' space,
I'm tauld are nocht but ba's o' fire;
An' gif that's sae, what needs my lyre
To strike her numbers 'mang the deid?
But thou, Carotus, tune my reed!
Thy airy umbels speak o' Life
Migrating aye thro' beauteous strife.
Thy gauzy petals far outrin
In mystery sweet the sun or muin;

But, yet, what beauty still I see
In thy fair brooch o' filigree—
Hoo witchin' it wad look gif press'd
On Queen Titania's bonnie breast!

But tell me whaur ye gat that gem—
That ruby rare—like diadem
Fair centred 'mang thy breathin' snaw,
Nae monarch ere wore ane sae braw?

I'd thocht ye were enou' adorned,
An' sic like jewels wad hae scorned.
Or art thou like dear ladies fair,
That to their charms maun add aye mair?
Maybe, like them, thou wadst decoy
The wee, fat, wing'd erotic boy
That, a' unseen, about their hearts
Twangs frae his bow his pleasing darts?
Or hast thou gat some queer ambition
To alter somewhat thy condition,
An' doff yer cloak that ermine shone,
An', Cæsar-like, the purple don?

Ae secret thou hast ne'er confess'd—
The plan ye tak' to big yer nest,
To bield yer bairns frae rain an' win',
Whan their wee sarks are bare an' thin!

I daurna bid ye be content—
Jist shift wi' thy ENVIRONMENT.

TO A SCOTCH THISTLE.

STRONG on thy sabred citadel,
  In power thou guard'st thy crimson crown !
What crawls, or creeps, or walks may tell
  The terrors of thy vengeful frown !

Long ere mankind had cut with stones,
  Or fair Damascus forged a blade,
Thy throne was girt with grins and groans !
  How many ages hast thou said—

" *Noli me tangere ?* " Say, what years,
  What cycles, did the Great Unseen
By Evolution forge the spears
  That fence thy towers of downy green ?

Far fairer flowers the herds entomb—
  As conquerors lay vain nations low—
Yet fearless waves thy ruby plume :
  And "Independence " still doth blow

Above thy sworded battlements,
  Like Britain's birthright !   May our isle,
Through direst days of red events,
  On Freedom's throne still proudly smile !

TO THE FORGET-ME-NOT.

(*Myasotis Palustris.*)

CERULEAN haunter of the rills :
   "Forget-me-not" thou need'st not say,
For thy rare beauty ever fills
   My mind with gladness while I stray
'Mong Meadow-sweet and Cuckoo flower,
To sanctify one Summer hour !

"Forget-me-not ; " thy petals blue,
   And pretty eye, seem sent to bless
The hearts of men that love the True,
   And all things beautiful caress :
By brooks that lave the mountain's brow
   A thing of dear delights art thou !

Sweeter than opening Eglantine
   Young Peggy tripping through the mead
To call, at early morn, the kine,
   Oft halts thy azure bloom to read,
Or plucks thee for her breast of snow,
With happy thoughts of Shepherd Joe !

In Winter wild, when thou art gone,
   To Fancy comes thy witching form.
Like Love's caress to maiden lone,
   Or like a sunbeam through the storm !
I nurse thee as a pleasing thought :
And *Legend*, flower, forgets thee not !

TO THE COMMON EYE-BRIGHT.

(*Euphrasia Officinalis.*)

WHEN wanderin' weary o'er the muir,
Whiles followed hard by clouds o' care,
Hoo aft I've marked thy bonnie e'e
Keek up as if to crack wi' me ;
Wee picture o' the purplin' dawn,
Fair pencilled by auld Nature's haun ;
What painter's art thy petals braw
Could e'er on plaque or canvas draw ?

Thy beauty—e'en aneath my lens—
Wad baffle twenty poets' pens,
Nor could the Muses in a ring
Thy sweetness and thy beauty sing.
By mountain path an' wimplin' burn
My een to thee wi' joy return,
Till, like yer ain, my e'e grows bright
Thou tiny source o' pure delight.

TO THE ROWAN TREE, OR MOUNTAIN ASH.

(Pyrus Aucuparia.)

THE strawberry keekin' frae saft, mossy dens,
The rasp droopin' sweet whaur the wild torrent stens,
The blaeberry hingin' the heather amang,
And the bramble's black e'e are a' worthy o' sang.
But amang thy wild crags thou art dearer to me
In thy bleeze o' red berries, my braw Rowan-tree.

Whaur the clear mountain burnies in Autumn saft sing,
There thy gay, scarlet clusters a' witchingly hing ;
An' the brawest aye dangle aboon the wild steep,
Like a maiden secure in a strong castle's keep ;
But ae sicht o' thy charms fills my heart fu' o' glee,
An' my haun' winna rieve thee—my braw Rowan-tree.

In the Spring when thy blossoms were scentin' the air,
Like a maid in her teens, thou wast tender and fair ;
But, buskit in green wi' the rose on thy cheek,
In Autumn nae brawer in woods could I seek ;
An' through the dark Winter a vision I'll see
O' the Simmer caressin' my braw Rowan tree.

THE TWO ROSES, OR SIMPLICITY.

WHAT beauty laves the lovely limbs
  Of sweet Simplicity !
Mark how she crowns yon fair wild Rose
  Throned on its thorny tree !
Then to the guarded garden turn,
  When roses flaunting blow
In all the pride of luxury
  And pomp of gaudy show.
My lady of Luxurious ease
  Calls them divinely fair,
And daily culls their fragrant forms
  To deck her soft Boudoir.
Yea, who may say the garden's queen
  Is not a flower complete,
To draw all men and maidens fair
  About her odour sweet ?
But mark the pamper'd Rose, when comes
  Her hour of swift decay :
Can this be she that proudly ruled
  O'er all the garden gay ?
A heap of foul deformity
  Falls on the fair green sward,
Telling how she, like mortals, reap
  High-living's sure reward ;
While from her wildling sister plain
  The fair-formed petals fall
In tender blushes down the dells,
  Like evening's purple pall.

And when October robes the woods
   In ruby, brown, and grey,
The Wild-rose decks her children * out
   The gayest of the gay.
O vagrant man ! this lesson learn—
   Pure, simple forms are best ;
And he who courts simplicity
   Obeys high heaven's behest.

---

* The Scarlet Hipps.

TO THE COMMON TORMENTIL.

(Potentilla Tormentilla : variety, Reptans.)

Was e'er the limbs of giddy Pompadour *
    Adorned with flowers so dainty or so neat
As you, reclining on this verdant floor,
    Unfolding thy soft charms so pure and sweet.

Thy quinate leaves and trailing form so fair,
    And yellow blooms of matchless symmetry,
Adorn this bank to kiss the lambent air,
    And o'er me throw a pleasing witchery.

With cunning art some painter may portray
    Thy graceful form ; but who may add the charms
That float about thee this sweet summer day,
    That holds all Nature in its loving arms ?

---

* She who captivated Louis XV. of France, was the first to intro-
duce dresses adorned with printed flowers.

TO THE COMMON MILK-WORT.

(Polygala Vulgaris.)

This sweet little haunter of our heathy pastures does her flirting in three different dresses—red, blue, and white: she has a decided preference, however, for the Imperial shade—blue.

SWEET lowly darling! Thou dost woo
   The moorlands' scanty green,
And greet'st the vagrant-winged cuckoo
   That ne'er hath Winter seen!

How prettily thou paint'st the grass
   With Red and Blue and White;
Thou'rt witching as a winsome lass,
   Or Fancy's fitful flight!

Bilberry blossoms, blushing, bend
   Above thy peerless gems:
Carnelians, Sapphires, Rubies, blend
   To beautify thy stems!

Like poet wandering far in dreams
   Soothed by the sound of rills,
So thou dost haunt the home of streams
   That silvery streak the hills!

TO THE GIANT BELL-FLOWER.

(*Campanula Latifolia.*)

WHILE down the glens the streams are singing
    Soft music to the fleecy flocks,
Thy little sisters sweet are ringing
    Their fairy bells around the rocks :

But here by gurgling Garnock's wave,
    (Thy airy form soft bowers concealing),
Fair Fancy doth my being lave,
    And thro' my soul thy bells are pealing !

Like regal guards the Foxgloves stand
    About thy towers of welkin blue ;
And Flora with her bounteous hand
    With thousand forms thy home doth strew.

Thy azure spires of breathing air,
    O'ercanopied by Woodbines twining,
From me dispel the city's care,
    And cleanse my heart from vain repining !

Here, 'neath thy wooded cloistered shade,
    Soothed with thy beauty, for a day—
I bless the Hand that hath thee made,
    And, grateful, homeward wend my way !

THE BOTANIST.

With Vasculum on shoulder, and his eyes
Like twin flowers, dew-lit, at the rosy dawn,
Forth walked the botanist: his was no march ;
But bee-like was his path among the flowers,
Drinking their loveliness.   A lonely man ?
O, no !   For his communings ever were
With earth's unnumbered stars—the spangled hosts
That stud the fields and kiss the brooks that sing
Adown the ferny glades.   To him came speech
And glance, from purple bloom and nectar'd bud
And glittering berry pendant on its stem.
The flower-bells seemed to ring within his soul
Soft chimes, while humble bombus all day bassed
To insect choirs on mead and moor.   His gaze
Was ever on the unsung wealth of flowers
That strewed his path : while Hope still led the way
To glad surprises in each new found form.
Crossing the snowy wreaths of clover soft
His heart rose heavenwards—for still he said
Their flakes, in love, from Paradise were blown,
Sweet with the angels' breath.
                        At eve I mark'd
The botanist towards the city wend—
His shoon with golden pollen powder'd o'er
By his belovéd flowers.   His garments bore
The perfumes of Queen Flora's banquet halls !
His lips betrayed the wild fruits' healing juice,
And e'en his breath told of Fragarian feasts
Spread on the mossy banks !

F

A peaceful joy
Sat on his rose-tipped cheeks—for had he not
Roamed through *his* garden broad of field and fen
Planted and pruned by His unerring hand
That lights heaven's myriad lamps, and paints so fair
The lily and the rose?
And I did hold
Him happier far than men who drudge and dream
Of wingèd wealth : for Nature was to him
A treasure that Old Time could never steal.

TO THE YELLOW GOAT'S-BEARD,

OR, "GO TO BED AT NOON, JACK."

(*Tragopogon Pratensis.*)

This strange plant, which belongs to the Dandelion family, closes its flower-head at noon—hence its English name. When rolled up in sleep, the Involucre resembles a goat's beard. Could the plant speak, it would tell a queer story anent its habit.

GONE to bed at noon, Jack?—
    Gone to bed at noon?
While the bees are humming
    Labour's sweetest tune.
You've not made your fortune—
    Why, then, bed so soon?
Up! the world is working—
    O, you lazy loon!

See, the flowers are vying
    Which shall kiss the sun;
All day they'll pursue him—
    Short race *you* have run!
Go and cut your goat's beard,
    Don your yellow vest;
Why, sir, prove a unit?
    Follow with the rest.

But, say, are you sleeping?
    Or do you count your gold
In some inner chamber,
    Where things manifold
Lie all about? My queer Jack,
    You seem a lazy loon;
But, maybe, there is wit, Jack,
    Within thy drowsy croon.

THE WILD THYME.

(*Thymus Serpyllum.*)

I CALL the hills a sanctuary,
　　Its Choristers, the Brooks ;
Its organ tone, the solemn Bee,
　　The flowers, its sacred Books ;
The azure sky, its dome sublime,
Its incense sweet, the fragrant Thyme.

TO THE SAME FLOWER.

AURORA sought thee on thy natal morn,
As on a mossy cradle softly lay
Thy slender stems : and, so, the goddess fair,
Soft kissing thee, did'st dower thee with her breath,
And blessed thee with the blushes of the dawn.

LINES

ON THE MONSTER ASH (FRAXINUS MONSTROSUS) GROWING IN THE KELVINGROVE PARK, GLASGOW.*

The queer looking forms left each year at the ends of the twigs of this tree are called fasciations. The exact cause of them has never been fully explained by botanists. If my readers think my muse has run riot in the following lines, let them go and inspect this strange production of nature for themselves. No charge—not even to people with a little fancy in their noddles.

O, THE strange Monster Ash, you can see't without cash,
　In the Kelvingrove Park, where it grows ;
For big girls and boys it hangs out its toys :
　Where it gets them—I wonder who knows ?
Look ! its queer fasciations, grow not by equations—
　You can see that quite plain where you stand—
Here's a butterfly's wing—there a bird that don't sing ;
　Why, some fairy's been here with her wand !
Here's an elfin-like fiddle, with the bridge in the middle,
　And volutes for capitals fair :
There's a head like a donkey—and yonder's a monkey
　On the end of a branch, I declare !
Here's Titania's harp—there, the tail of a carp,
　(Give your fancy fair play for a smile),
Look ! as sure's I'm a Scot, that's the oar of a boat,
　Greek helmets, and forms versatile !
And, see you, man, look ! there's a shepherd's bold
　　crook,
　Don't you fancy you hear his dog bark ?
See what this twig is holding—why, some fairy's been
　　moulding
　The great dorsal fin of a shark !

---

* This ash must be seen before its leaves cover the last year's growths.

Now, say, did I lark, to ask you to the park
   To shew you these freaks all so queer,
Growing up on a tree, as your fancy can see ?
   But they'll all be transformed by next year.
All poets declare that Nature is fair—
   Yet many odd forms she doth toss us ;
Now, between you and me, the full name of that tree
   Is (note it) *Fraxinus Monstrosus !* "

LINES ON A FIELD OF WHITE CLOVER.

(Trifolium Repens.)

RICH—not rare—not a gaudy show,
    But with joy I tread it over :
Each pretty ball like a flake of snow—
    'Tis only a field of clover ;
Yet, O my heart, thy all now yield
And say—" 'Tis mine, this *treasure* field ! "

Away from the city's sloughs and slums,
    I list to lessons sober—
From morn till eve the hive bee hums
    'Mong the wreaths of creamy clover ;
Like Love's fond message from o'er the sea
Is the perfume pure of this clover lea.

I hold all worldly wealth in scorn,
    And Care—thou hearts' corroder—
Rise thou not with this July morn
    On this milky mead of clover !
But come all peaceful thoughts and rare
And revel free in its fragrant air !

O, sweet is a kiss in a rosy bower,
    To lips with longing weary ;
And sweet are wells at the noonday hour
    To men in deserts dreary ;
But with purer joys my mind runs over
When zephyrs waft me the scent of clover.

TO THE WHITE WATER-LILY.

(*Nymphea Alba.*)

HAIL, lovely Nymph of the limpid lake!
　On the deep blue waters you set your throne;
O, I know not if I should the silence break
　That reigns by the shore where I wander lone.
Can the muse be mute while thy snowy rim
To the organ tones of the bee doth hymn?

O, the spirit of Beauty my fancy sees
　In thy silvery lamp with its golden flame,
As it floateth so fair, with its witcheries,
　And my lingering eyes still seem to claim—
Till they join with the ripples that dancing play
Round your fairy form, keeping holiday.

I may cull the Rose, but her thorn must bear,
　Though her perfumed breath be a balm to heal;
Though Camelia flaunt in my true love's hair,
　No odours sweet doth her form reveal;
But thou thy beauty and breath dost keep,
For they reign and ride on the waters deep.

TO THE GOLDEN SAXIFRAGE.

(Chrysosplenium Oppositifolium.)

By todlin' burns, whaur birdies sing
To welcome mossy sandalled Spring ;
Whaur rocks wi' dewy diamonds hing—
    Whaur torrents rage—
There in thy beauty thou dost cling,
    Gay Saxifrage !

Adorner o' the rifted glen,
Aye hauntin' whaur clear waters sten,
By monie a sweet wee cosie den
    I see thy form,
In gowden brooch come steppin' ben
    Frae Winter's storm.

Whaur water kelpies sit and gaze
In crystal linns, thro' April days ;
Whaur siller fountains gem the braes,
    Thy beauty's spread ;
Or whaur some singing cascade plays
    Aroun' thy bed.

Hoo bonnilie thou fling'st a spell
O' verdure roun' some mountain well,
Where aft I've sat, as evening fell,
    By its gurgling brim,
To list what my puir Muse wad tell
    For my next hymn.

TO THE BUTTERCUPS OR KINGCUPS.

(Ranunculus Acris.)

YE are sure of rich degree—
Flora's goldsmiths may ye be ?
Or do ye bear her royal wine
In your cups of wealthy shine ?

Wayside flowers I know ye are,
Each resplendent as a star ;
Yet within your goblets glossy
Lies a pleasure for wee Flossy,
Betty, Tommy, Ted, and Bill,
As their tiny hands they fill
With your gold, that brings them joy—
Happiness without alloy.

Ah ! I see ye every year,
Shining in your splendour clear,
Like a golden coronet
Round young Summer's temples set ;
And my soul in silence sups
Plenitudes from out your cups ;
And I am a child again,
Romping careless down the lane.

BELLS.

(The Flower-lover's Version.)

In purple and gold, in beauty untold,
  Far away o'er the moor ye are ringing ;
And deep in the dells where the pure torrent swells,
  And deep in my soul ye are singing.

O, sweet flowery bells, O soft toning bells,
  On the ear of fair Fancy ye chime :
Ye were cast in dull earth, and the sun gave ye birth
  And your beauty begetteth my rhyme !

O, the woods are all ringing with Hyacinths swinging
  Sweet odours aloft to the dove ;
While, meek in the shade, the Primrose like a maid
  Seems silently dreaming of Love !

From its spire of great bells, the Foxglove aye tells
  That its temple lies ope for the bee :
Hark ! she hummeth a prayer, and entereth there
  'Neath a crimson and gold canopy !

'Mong the fields and the flowers, by the rills, among
    bowers
  I have joys that court me unbidden ;
In these are my wealth, never pilfered by stealth,
  Tho' to many they ever lie hidden !

TO THE RAGWORT.

(Senecio Jacobœa.)

This plant will seek lea fields, although the farmer wages incessant war against it.   Hennedy says—"A good crop with bad farmers."

RAGWORT, thou art a sturdy loon !
  What tho' the farmer's sickle keen,
Lays low thy spreading yellow croon,
  Still o'er his rigs thy form is seen.

Thou maun ha'e pith within thy pow
  Tae warsle 'gainst sic sneddin' fate :
I won'er that ye dinna vow
  Frae fickle fields to tak' the gate,

An' plant yersel' whaur cruel steel
  Ne'er shears yer shanks—whaur void o' fear
Yer ruggit, tawted tap may feel
  Some wimplin' burnie roun' it steer.

Ragwort, yer like the honest puir
  That haud their ain whate'er betide ;
That, somehoo, thrive 'mid hardships sair,
  An' o'er Life's billows couthie ride.

An' when to Death they pay the kine,
  Like thee they leave a buirdly race
Firm planted—for a haun Divine
  For ilk thing leevin' has a place !

TO THE SEA-PINK.

(Armeria Vulgaris.)

WHERE Neptune flings his briny spray
Athwart the rocks, thou noddest gay ;
Upon the tottering tawny brink
Of giddy crags, there blooms thy pink !

Where calm in coves the waters lie,
Like pretty patches of the sky,
I love to mark thy form recline,
Or in the azure mirror shine !

Thy image makes me ever glad
While wandering by the sea-shore sad ;
Thy beauty, like a gleam of light,
Makes all the dull grey shingle bright !

If round a country-garden bed
I see thy purple blossoms spread,
My fancy seawards flies once more,
And hears the breakers beat the shore !

STARS.

WHEN winter wraps the earth in cold,
The heavenly hosts their fires unfold ;
The city of the mighty One
Is bathed in light—each lamp a sun !
Then Fancy, with her nimble feet,
May pace far down each golden street,
Or tread, all wonder-robed, alone
The precincts of Jehovah's throne !

One night, lone musing on my way,
Through orbed space my eye did stray ;
The Dog star like a diamond skinkled,
While countless galaxies all twinkled
In many a beauteous scintillation
Around Orion's constellation,
As when the seer of Uz did turn
His awe-struck gaze to see them burn
Above his tents, when earth was young,
'Ere yet the shepherd King had sung
The praise of Him whose word did frame
That wondrous universe of flame.
Ah ! had the royal bard's quick eye
Seen fairy Science sweep the sky
With optic glass and Reason's ken,
What peans he had poured then
To Israel's God !

O, dreadful space !—
Methinks the Almighty's awful face
Looks down from His eternal throne

On man, His image—gazing lone
Into His courts ! This is too vast—
Amid His shoreless sea I'm cast !

From rolling suns my reason turns
To this that in me ever burns—
The Mind of man, more wondrous still—
The mind that doth Creation fill ;
How truly Zion's singer said—
" Thou hast but little lower made
Man than Thyself ! " *   O wonder this
That 'mid God's wonders oft we miss !

From heavenly stars, on downward wing,
To earth I turn.   'Tis balmy Spring ;
The fields with living stars are gay,
My feet traverse the Milky-way
Of dewy daisies—each a sun
That still its beauteous course doth run
Beneath the great All-seeing Eye
That studs with gems the midnight sky.

How spangled lovely earth is seen,
In silver, gold, and varied green !
Dear earth-born stars, I turn to you !—
To you my simple lays renew !
Heaven's fiery hosts God's might aye prove ;—
Ye are the reflex of His love.
Gay *living* forms—more beauteous far
Than sun or moon or gem-like star.

---

* The correct rendering of the Hebrew in Psalm viii., 6, I am told,
is, " Thou hast made him a little lower than Thyself."

TO AN UNTIMELY ROSE,

THAT WOULD BLOOM LATE IN DECEMBER, BUT WAS NIPP'D BY THE FROST.

WAN wanderer in a weary waste,
　　Far from thy summer home,
I mourn to mark thy drooping form
　　'Neath winter's murky dome.

What waked thee from thy restless sleep ?
　　Heard'st thou the zephyr's tone,
That spake of warmth and sunny smiles
　　From sunlit seas upborne ?

Frail sister of the fragrant queen,
　　The poetry of flowers,
Nipp'd by the north ; thy scentless bloom
　　Frozen by icy showers.

Ah ! type of beauty robed in pride,
　　That ruin still o'ercomes,
That leaves her summer mansion fair,
　　To perish in the slums !

Far from thy home!　My being bleeds
　　To see thee pine and die,
While, lov'd, thy sister's cheeks shall blush
　　Beneath June's azure sky.

Envoi.

Untimely flower !　To me thou art
　　Like laughter round the grave,
Or like a gem that mocking decks
　　The shackles of a slave !

LINES ON THE YELLOW FIELD-CRESS.

(*Nasturtium Sylvestris.*)

This trailing plant, with its exquisite leaves and profusion of bright golden blossoms, is rarely found in Scotland, and then it is usually adorning some waste place or heap of rubbish. I have come across it in several spots 30 miles round Glasgow, and in each case it was on a railway—often close to the track or on a little-used siding.

As rushed the train, (like comet bold),
　Along its path of steel,
I chanced to spy a patch of gold—
A flower of beauty manifold—
　Close by Destruction's wheel.

And marking quick the spot, as one
　Who finds a treasure rare—
When labour's hours their course had run,
Ere yet had set the Summer sun—
　I found my beauty fair.

And, lo, it was the Field Cress bright,
　Its bed the dull gray dross,
Yet radiant now with golden light,
Resplendent as the brow of night
　Gemmed with the Southern Cross.

On rubbish heaps this flower doth blow—
　Makes spots, despised and mean,
With brighter gold than Ophir glow,
And barren places oftimes show
　The pageant of a queen.

Thus oft we see, in slums and lanes,
　Fair Virtue sweetly bloom ;
And 'mid a city's sins and pains
Hear Charity, in dulcet strains,
　Come piping through the gloom.

TO THE WILD STRAWBERRY.

(*Fragaria Vesca.*)

WHEN the banks and dells are dight
　With the moonlit Primrose gay,
Then thy stars so snowy white
　Seem to twinkle and to say :—
" We do shine thine eyes to greet,
But we herald promise sweet."

When the June sun waxeth hot,
　And the torrent turns a rill,
'Tis the schoolboys' happy lot
　Joyously to roam at will,
Or loll upon each mossy bed
Plucking thy luscious berries red !

Though sager grown, I deem it bliss
　To join their rambles—pleased to glean
Thy fragrant fruit, rare as the kiss—
　The first pure kiss of sweet eighteen !
Thy sisters gross, in gardens placed,
Lack thy simplicity and taste !

TO THE BARREN-STRAWBERRY.

(*Potentilla Fragariastrum.*)

It requires the experienced eye of the botanist to discern the differ-
ence between the leaves and flowers of this plant and the true strawberry. As it name implies, it bears no berries—only seeds like the
other Potentillas.

THE botanist, he knows you well,
White peeping in some woody dell ;
But, plodding hard, he may not tell
　　Thy history queer :
Why unto fruit thou dost not swell,
　　The birds to cheer !

The children, nesting in the Spring,
Delighted hear the blackbird sing,
And, spying you, their hopes take wing—
　　They mark thy bed ;
Their pretty lips in fancy wring
　　Sweet berries red !

And, when hot panting June comes round,
They seek thy home—they know the ground ;
To guarded spots they joyous bound—
　　But, sad surprise !
Thy mocking leaves alone are found
　　To dim their eyes !

Thou'rt just like folk that only talk :
In mimic leaves and flowers they walk ;
With pretty speech they cunning balk
　　Old Want and Woe ;
Their charity is writ in chalk—
　　No fruit they show !

LINES TO AN OLD GOOSEBERRY BUSH

IN A CERTAIN GARDEN.

The author, when a boy, often had Sulphur Grossets off this bush, and it is still bearing abundance of fruit, tho' said to be over seventy years old.

THO' guid, douce John an' Mary Hortle
Ha'e lang since pass'd Death's dreary portal,
Yet thy auld form, grown horizontal,
  Aye seems to me
A thing that I might ca' immortal—
  That canna dee.

When thy wee blossoms sweet did hing,
On sunny days, in balmy Spring,
I've marked the bees on early wing,
  I, tho' a birkie,
Wad listen lang to hear them sing
  Like some wee kirkie.

At Fair time I kept sweet wi' Mary—
She yont the orchard kept a dairy—
She'd gar me doff my auld Glengary,
  Syne, roun' thee happin',
Frae thee she'd pou, large, ripe an' hairy,
  A big Scotch chappin.

Then aff I'd toddle, fu' o' glee,
Nae monarch hauf sae proud as me,
As, squatted 'neath the auld Aik tree,
  I feasted fine ;
An' thocht nae royal dish could be
  Sae gran' as mine !

Let southern bards Parnassus spiel,
An' sing hoo Grapes in humplocks reel
In fizzin' vats—I'll say't—a Deil
      Is in ilk berry ;
Wine gars puir dottards downward squeel
      Tae Charon's ferry !

An' tho' at times we pree the Grape,
Its seeds like stanes aft gar us gape,
As 'mang auld stumps we howk an' scrape
      Wi' pin an' picker—
Till Beauty's face taks monie a shape
      While loonies titter !

Let me the juicy Grosset praise :
When ripe its gat nae tricky ways,
Nae surfeit on oor painch it lays—
      Nor grips, nor bile ;
I wish the Grosset length o' days
      In oor bless'd isle !

If Luxury an' Wealth maun ban us
Wi' trashtry frae the het Havanahs,
Their Melons, Pomegranates, Bananas—
      Wi' fumes like Rosset :
Still may the Powers aboon aye staun us
      The halesome Grosset !

BOTANY AND RAILWAY BANKS.

If, in the British Isles, population, house and factory building, and laying out of cemeteries go on increasing at the rate they have been doing during the past twenty years, we may have few spots left as homes for our wild flowers; and it seems to me that our railway embankments will be the custodians of nine-tenths of our wild flora.

THE farmer turns his furrows o'er,
　　The cattle and the sheep must graze,
And fruity orchards, more and more
　　Do widen, in these sumptuous days:
Where shall I turn for wild-flower ways?
　　Death takes his acres, with no thanks,
And fainter falls the field flowers' blaze:
　　　There's one rich band, where science clanks,
　　　And Flora courts the Railway banks!

Here neither plough nor scythe can mar
　　The beautiful, the rich, the rare:
The floral gem, the living star,
　　The sweet-breathed, chafing Summer's air!
At, just say fourteen miles—nae mair—
　　As on the steel steed snorting spanks—
On holidays I sit and stare
　　　On one long garden; and my thanks
　　　Ascend to heaven for Railway banks!

THE ACORN.

(A Rhyme for the Children.)

WHILE roaming in a wood, one day,·
   A boy on an Acorn trod :
And thus that orb of life did say—
   "Through Winter cold, beneath this sod,
I'll sleep, till Spring his bugle blow,
To banish north the frost and snow.

Two rounded blades I'll then unfold,
   Then tiny leaves to shew my race—
That I have sprung from monarchs old :
   My impy form will fill small space,
Until a hundred years are fled,
And thou art sleeping with the dead !

And then perhaps thy grandson may
   (As truant, 'neath my boughs, he wipes
The sweat of fear) when Hyps look gay,
   Climb up my arms to gather Pipes.*
Yea, while man's generations go,
A sturdy oak I still shall grow.

And while great Kings shall rise and reign,
   And Empires like old sabres rust,
My power shall spread with might and main,
   While cities proud are razed to dust—
Until some day the woodman's blow
Shall lay my spreading glory low !

---

* The calyx or cup that holds the acorn.

And, after that, my limbs may rear
   A school to train a Shakespere's mind,*
And pilgrims come from year to year
   Sweet inspiration there to find :
And my strong arms may bear afar,
On thundering ships, old Britain's star !

So, little deeds of kindness done,
   And simple words, if dropp'd in love,
May grow in might, when thou hast won
   Thy crown of life in Heaven above :—
Despise not aught that's small—if TRUE :—
Mont Blanc himself from atoms grew ! "

---

* The Grammar School at Stratford, where Shakespere was educated, was founded by Edward VI.—and is still a school : the strong beams that keep it together are of oak: and very likely young William played over them.

TO THE CORN-FLOWER.

(Centauria Cyanus.)

DECKED in dainty frills of blue,
   'Mong the Corn you flirt and play :
And, for lover, none will do,
   Save the Scarlet Poppy gay !

Complement'ry—blue and red—
   Ye each other's charms enhance ;
When to blending were ye bred ?
   Long, long ago ; and not by chance !

Pretty children's willing feet
   Dare not roam where you do grow ;
For among the farmer's wheat
   Quite secure your blossoms blow.

As a lovely lady fair
   Smiteth from her castle walls,
And no love-sick knight may dare
   Follow where her footstep falls :

So, from out the golden corn,
   Thou dost throw thy azure charms ;
And, until of beauty shorn,
   Thou art safe from rude alarms.

TO THE BIRD'S-FOOT TREFOIL.

(Lotus Corniculatus.)

THOUGH lowly guise thou dost assume,
Thou art a rival of the Broom,
And Thymy knolls for thee make room—
    Lotus Corniculatus !

Thy dainty petals, tipp'd with red,
By sunbeams of the springtime fed,
Are quick in yellow beauty spread—
    Lotus Corniculatus !

And when thou spread'st thy golden shields,*
And turn'st to Ophir lanes and fields—
What dear delights thy treasure yields—
    Lotus Corniculatus !

With thy rich beauty in mine eye,
How sweet it is, in June, to lie
And list the Minstrel of the sky—
    Lotus Corniculatus!

One day with thee, 'mong bleating flocks,
And cascades reeking down the rocks—
Is rare respite to city folks—
    My thanks, Corniculatus !

---

* If any fail to realise the figure here used, let them visit the sandy pastures of the Ayrshire coast during the summer, where they will see rounded patches of this lovely flower forming golden shields from 1 to 3 feet diameter.

TO THE COMMON VETCH.

(Vicia Angustifolia.)

This pretty ruby-coloured flower, which grows on sandy pastures, is the origin of the cultivated Vetch with which every schoolboy is acquainted.

WHEN smiling May, in golden crown,
   And mantle of the milky thorn,
Comes in her rich flower-dappled gown,
   Sparkling with dew drops of the morn,
One Ruby rare adorn'st her brow—
And, lowly floweret, it is thou !

Among the gay green tender grass,
   It glads my heart to see thee shine !
A gem like you I ne'er could pass,
   And I, tho' poor, may call thee mine !
The jewels sordid wealth can buy,
Ne'er kindled fire in poet's eye !

THE CHRYSANTHEMUM SHOW IN THE BOTANIC GARDENS, GLASGOW.

NOVEMBER, 1896.

Dedicated to Mr. Dewar, curator of the Gardens, who is deserving
of the thanks of the whole city and suburbs for his annual exhibition
of these lovely flowers.

Wi' ither folk the Muse e'en comes,
An' to Saint Mungo saftly hums
Her bonnetted Chrysanthemums
  Frae queer Japan;
An' on their beauty tries her thrums
  As best she can !

Aneath the Kibble's ample shade,
In close battalions a' arrayed,
Like Grenadiers on high parade
  Afore the Queen;
Or some enchantin' masquerade
  To feast her een !

Or might I ca't a galaxie
O' ladies cled harmoniouslie—
Ilk ane o' noble pedigree
  In Court or ha',
Turned oot to fling warm witcherie
  O'er Winter's snaw ?

Their walth on dress they dinna spare—
Here's ane in gowd like millionaire—
See, this ane spreads her bosom fair
  Like lily white;
While some their royal bluid declare
  In purple bright !

Some blush like sunsets—some hae strains
O' azure hair bells i' their veins:
Some bronz'd, as if o'er Afric's plains
      They lang had trod—
Bearing sweet spices in their trains
      To waft abroad !

In sweet accord, on Dewar's tower,
A' thae gar youth and beauty glower ;
An' civic rulers feel what power
      In concord lies :—
On each the heavens a charm doth shower
      Frae kindly skies !

Dewar, thy bonnie flowers aye preach,
An' auld Saint Mungo's bairnies teach,
That wad their city aiblins reach
      PROSPERITY,
Nae ane maun ower the ither streetch—
      But a' agree !

TO THE PHEASANT'S EYE, OR POET'S LILY.

(Narcissus Poeticus.)

RICH treasury of heaven's balmy air,
    Soft, silver-spangled spoiler of the sun,
The poet's lily—fairest of the fair—
    What love and music hath thy beauty won !

Fair image of celestial loveliness !
    The fingers of young Innocence alone
May dare to touch thee, or, in love, caress
    Thy beauty, when thy breathing snow is blown.

What tho' day's orb warm woos thee with his beams,
    On thy chaste cheek he ne'er shall raise a blush ;
And tho' thy fragrance haunts the poet's dreams,
    Thy snowy sanctity his harp might hush.

Fair flitteth Fancy thro' her airy halls,
    When sings the throstle after vernal showers ;
But thy pure splendour every sense enthrals—
    Thou art the vestal princess of the flowers.

TO THE MEADOW CRANE'S-BILL.

(Geranium Pratensé.)

This is by far the handsomest of all our wild Geraniums.

THE Woodbine from her golden horn
Pours incense on the wings of morn
Where thy soft purple bloom was born—
      Geranium Pratensé.

Free, up the trouty stream I roam,
Where waters leap in fretful foam,
Where you and Fancy make your home—
      Geranium Pratensé.

How sweet by singing brooks to lie,
'Neath humming woods in hot July,
Thy handsome blossoms in my eye—
      Geranium Pratensé.

Thy southern sisters move elate
In scarlet robes and pride of state
About the mansions of the great—
      Geranium Pratensé.

There, 'neath hot glassy shades up-pent,
Their languorous sickly days are spent:—
But, give me thy Environment—
      Geranium Pratensé :—

The sighing Birk, the fragrant Rose,
The vocal woods—the dear repose
That Nature o'er her lover throws—
      Geranium Pratensé.

LINES

To an Artificial Rose Adorning a Lady's Golden Hair.*

What a triumph of Art on a throne of gold!
O, where is the poet, or young or old,
Will sing of the fingers so dainty and neat
That can mimic the queen of all flowerets sweet?
The chisel and brush wake the poet's fires,
But what bold singer to her aspires
That set thy red petals and leaves and stems
And even thy anthers like golden gems?
No muse of mine shall thy beauty mar—
Thou, near unto Nature, yet from her so far!
Fair mimic, adorning a brow of snow,
Thou bearest the form of the real that blow
In my lady's garden in noonday pride—
When the Honeysuckles their blushes hide!
Ah, must I call thee a counterfeit
Of the flower of Love—so fair and fleet?
Thou art set as a charm 'mong my lady's locks
Where Cupid still hides 'mong their golden flocks.
The wildling Rose to the bee is a spell;
But thou, where thou art, ah! my heart knows well!
O, wert thou, lady, for me so fair,
And thy bosom the love of mine could share,
I would gather thee roses gemmed with dew,
And like thy fair cheek, of a peachy hue;
I would gather thee buds when the morning drips,
And Aurora is kissing their crimson lips!

---

* Why the painters of flowers should be lauded and well paid, and the poor girls who make artificial ones (with such cunning as to deceive our very senses), should be left out in the cold and paid wages that can barely keep body and soul together, I cannot understand. Ladies —think of this!

FERNS.

ADORERS of the regal woods!
  What tho' no flowers adorn
Your palmy grace and symmetry—
  Ye are of Beauty born:
I deem ye still the fairest things
That deck the glades or crystal springs!

How gracefully your palmy fronds
  Adorn the forest fanes,
Or waving o'er some mountain brook
  Ye waft the Throstle's strains;
Or down the glen your tender green
  Throws round the linn a fairy sheen!

Did Mother Nature ere unfold
  Forms fairer of design
Than yours, gay ferns? Your loveliness
  Speaks of the Hand Divine!
O, while I tread this beauteous Earth,
  Of joy my heart need dread no dearth!

TO THE FRAGRANT GYMNADENIA.

(AN ORCHID.)

(*Gymnadenia Conopsea.*)

O'ER heathy pastures, where the sheep
   Like distant boulders seem,
I seek thy perfumed purple form,
   As miser in a dream,
Lone, gathers Ophir's yellow ore,
And, happy, heaps his hidden store.

How sweet, in June, thy balmy breath
   About the upland rills,
When globe-flowers light the rushy mead,
   And larks sing o'er the hills ;
And Joy and I for miles might stray,
To feel thy breath in evening grey.

Thy Orchidacean sisters fair
   We bring from sunnier lands,
And bind their beauty all about
   With artificial bands ;
Yet hear what one, thy singer, saith—
"They all may envy thy sweet breath."

Yea, Love through thy pure odour wings
   His tender flight ; he steals
About thy fragrant blooms, but still
   His awful form conceals ;
And when, dear flower, I seek for thee
My heart aye fills with charity.

TO THE GARDEN NASTURTIUM, OR INDIAN-CRESS.

(Tropiolum Majus.)

This garden favourite, that blooms on till frosts nip it, is named Nastartium from the pungent taste of its seeds, and leaves as well— the word literally meaning "The Nose Twitcher." Its specific name, Tropiolum, means Trophies—its leaf resembling a shield and the flower a helmet.

IMPERIAL flower of warmth and light :
Thou had'st not aye that helmet bright,
But won thy trophies fair in fight
      Through æons lone,
And now thou hold'st, by sovereign right,
      Thy fiery throne.

In flaming folds of floral fire,
To bind my bower's thy one desire ;
And there thy hues, like sweetest choir,
      Harmonious blend—
There, till October's tints expire,
      Thy beauty spend.

In spring, the Lily fragrance throws—
In Summer blooms the queenly Rose ;
But, when the mellow Apple shows
      Her blushes fair,
Loved Mignonette about thee blows
      Her perfume rare.

And bright the Gladiolus rears,
To guard thy throne, his mighty spears :
And Love his potent shaft oft clears
  By thy warm glow,
Behind thy shields young Hope oft hears
  His twanging bow !

When friends of youth, and manhood's stay,
Like flowers in Spring and Summer gay
By Time's fierce blast are borne away
  Far from my view,
Heaven grant—to cheer Life's closing day—
  A friend like you !

TO THE SCARLET PIMPERNEL, OR POOR MAN'S WEATHER-GLASS.

(*Anagallis Arvensis.*)

If this pretty little plant could speak it would tell us that its reason
for closing its cup before rain is to preserve its pollen, and so perpetuate its name : in short—like a true redcoat it keeps its powder dry,
and has, consequently, a better chance for its life.

THOU dost not flaunt thy flaming flag
    If rain is drawing near ;
And dost not count among thy friends
    Soft showers, that bring good cheer.

I know you keep your table bright
    And shining, for the flies—
And so you keep a sharp look out
    For murky drizzling skies.—

'Twould never do to cheat your guests
    Of sweets and pollen yellow ;
And, wise, you keep your cupboard dry,
    My thrifty little fellow !

And so, while blessing others, you
    Still think of your descendants ;
So that your ancient name may live
    With train of poor dependants.

But when your banner is unfurled
    It is a pretty sight
To see the green and tender grass
    Gleam with its scarlet bright.

My tender barometric friend—
  Wee pretty weather glass—
Your sense of feeling must be fine,
  And mine must far surpass !

I would that you could speak, wee flower,
  And give a retrospection
Of how you came to read the skies
  With such a rare perfection !

TO THE COMMON CENTAURY.

(Erythrea Centaurium.)

This flower is also a sun wooer, and avoids rain. It grows in great
beauty and abundance on the sand dunes by the sea shore at Port Rush.

PINKY wooer of the sun !
　　When he smileth thou art gay :
'Neath his glory thou wilt run,
　　Red robed, all a Summer's day.

When the lord of day doth hide
　　Under rain clouds, then in fear
Well thou knowest he doth chide,
　　And thou mourn'st his absent cheer.

Thou art of the thoughtful flowers—
　　Tho' perhaps a little shy—
For thou seem'st to know the hours
　　To follow—whether WET or DRY.

Often in my summer walks
　　I will stand and read thy face ;
And upon thy tapered stalks
　　Coming showers can oft times trace.

Pretty rover of the dunes,
　　Thy tiny candelabra bright
In my bosom wake soft tunes—
　　Kindle there a pure delight !

Purple thyme about thee blows—
  Soothed I press its fragrant sod—
And here and there a Burnet Rose
  Odour sheds where violets nod.

These, thy rare companions meet,
  Carpeting the sand dunes' floor ;
Perhaps with me they come to greet
  Thy beauty by the murm'ring shore.

TO THE GREAT CONVOLVULUS.

(Calystegia Sepium.)

This plant, although it bears a really beautiful flower, is universally detested for its utter selfishness; for in order to show off its white bells, it not only tramples over all obstacles in its upward growth, but spreads its root stems far and wide underground—causing general destruction to beauty and utility—a type, surely, of pride and sordid ambition.

TYPE of sordid, vain Ambition!
  Fairest flower nor breathing Briar
Work in thee a heart contrition :—
  Thou'rt for self—so, higher, higher,
Till thy bells of shining snow
"Victory" peal o'er all below!

Every height must have its hollow!
  So, when surly Winter calls,
In his train thou need'st must follow—
  At his feet thy beauty falls;
While the humble Daisy's rays
· Help to cheer December's days!

Pride, self-twining, oft doth climb,
  Heartless still, o'er honest worth;
But the withering breath of Time
  Lays all transient show in earth :—
The man is bless'd, thrice happy he,
Who daily courts Humility!

LINES

TO A YELLOW JESSAMINE IN FLOWER ON A COTTAGE
WALL NEAR AYR, DECEMBER, 1894.

THERE! like a happy thought, to light
  The Poet, ere the Muses sleep,
I mark thy yellow blossoms bright,
  About this cottage window creep!

Kissing the Frost's ephemeral leaves
  Upon the panes, thy wealth of youth
Perchance for soft-winged Love still grieves—
  Still sigheth for thy sunnier South.

Rare picture thou, of living gold,
  Thy setting soft—the silvery snow;
Thou flowery flame 'mid Winter's cold—
  My heart warms at thy kindly glow!

As dulcet music thralls the ear,
  Thy beauty captive keeps my eye;
With thee all Summer's sounds I hear,
  And Broomy June goes humming by!

TO THE WILD ROSE.

(*Rosa Canina.*)

SWEET Rose ! thy native air is song :
  And well the poet saith
That Love, the ever young and strong,
  Still breatheth in thy breath.

When first the Flower of Ocean's foam *
  With light foot touched the land,
She sought beneath thy shade a home,
  And smote thee with her wand ;
And quick thy perfumed petals flew
  About her form so fair,
Till sleep his silent curtains drew
  About her golden hair.
So first on bed of Roses slept
  The queen of Love's great power ;
And well her wingéd son hath kept
  The fragrance of that hour :

For swift from out thy opening buds
  In odour Cupid flies—
His wings adorned with dewy studs,
  The light of maidens' eyes !

Sweet Rose—the Poetry of flowers—
  Still to the Muses dear :
Thou art, within thy thorny bowers,
  The glory of the year !

---

* Venus.

TO MAY, 1896.

In the memory of the oldest, there has not been seen such a profusion of Hawthorn blossom as in the present month. This flower, with others, is also about three weeks earlier than usual.

I GREET thee, queen month of the year ! Hail, May !
   Thy fragrant mantle of the creamy thorn
Methinks ne'er spread so ample or so gay
   As now in Ninety-six. At early morn
I wander 'mong the lanes, to quaff the scent
   Of thine own blossom ; and afar and near
The air is redolent. I, city pent,
   With rapture the sweet Throstle's piping hear !
Where'er I turn thy Hawthorn I descry
   Like snowy wreaths ; and every field is gay
With Daisy constellations ; so that I
   Seem roaming in the moonlight during day.

TO THE CORN MARIGOLD.

(*Chrysanthemum Segetum.*)

My Fancy never groweth old
　To meet thee 'mong the ripening corn,
Arrayed in thy gay garb of gold
　Where Plenty fills her Autumn horn :

And when the sickle steals thy crown,
　And all the barns are big with grain,
Among the tubered fields so brown
　Thy beauty hails me once again :

So winsome, bonnie, blithe, and gay !
　October greets thee, sad and sere ;
Her falling tresses round thee play—
　Bright rearguard of the floral year !

Ev'n when November's sun is low
　And Winter flaps his fleecy wings,
Thy gold among his silvery snow
　A solace in the sadness brings.

When Flora lays her treasures past—
　Till Spring shall call (her wooer bold)
Her golden crown she placeth last ;
　And thou art it—Corn Marigold !

TO THE KNAPWEED, OR STAR-THISTLE.

(Centaurea Nigra.)

I.

I MAY not call you a lovely plant—
    For your beauty is all on your bonnet ;
So my jaded Muse she need not pant
    To shew you off in a sonnet !
But I'll lilt you a song on this moorland road,
    While the kindly breezes whistle
Right over your purple crown, so broad—
    Frail mimic of Scotland's Thistle ! *

II.

Your unsavoury stem hath no need of spears
    Like the Thistles—green and sappy :
But you steer your way thro' the strife of years,
    And you always look quite happy
In your rosy head-gear—bobbing about
    'Mong Hair-bells blue, and Bedstraw yellow,
While the dainty Eyebright peepeth out
    As if to say—" you're a handsome fellow ! "

III.

When the July days are hot and still,
    And the wild-fruit time is coming ;
Then I pensive stray by some tinkling rill
    Where the moorland bees are humming
About your crimson bloom—like bells
    Far off, in a Sabbath gloaming :
And I bless your bonnet and all its spells—
    For I'm wed to my wild-flower roaming !

---

* It has no thorns.

TO THE BOG-BEAN.

(*Menyanthes Trifoliatum.*)

O, RAREST work of Nature's deft design !
  O peerless princess in Queen Flora's halls !
Thy snowy loveliness who may define ?
  Soft beauty reigns where'er thy footstep falls.

Like silvered candelabra round the lake,
  Thy fairy lights illume the rushy mead ;
While cherub Larks above thee music wake,
  And, flushed, Aurora to the Day doth speed !

Lov'd Menyanthes ! Thou art angel fair !
  I dare not cull thee by this trickling brook,
Nor bind thee in my true love's raven hair,
  But gaze on thee—then to thy Maker look !

FLORA.

ONCE the Lily and the Rose
    Would their mutual sweetness lend
To some spot of soft repose,
    Where their lovely hues might blend :—
He who would the fair ones seek,
Woos sweet Flora's neck and cheek.

The Bramble sighed to Love's young lord,
    "Must my glittering glory fade ?
Is my witchery ignored ?
    I'll enrich this beauteous maid."
Cupid claiming such a prize,
Changed the blobs to Flora's eyes !

Thus on young Flora beauty showers
From Autumn's fruit and Summer's flowers.

THE LILY AND THE ROSE.

A FABLE.

CUPID, winging through the air,
Lighted in a garden fair—
Soft, between that lovely pair,
    The Lily and the Rose.
Slumber laved his wondrous eyes,
But with a sudden new surprise
He started—hearing sobs and sighs
    That troubled his repose.

For the flowers of Love and Song
Mourned "The gods have done us wrong,
That we should bloom amid a throng
    Of flowers of low degree !
O, Love ! thou heat from heaven's fire,
To follow thee we twain aspire ;
O, Cupid, grant us this desire—
    We would immortal be !"

The god of Love quick culled the twain,
And, with soft music in his train,
He flew afar o'er land and main
    To choose a spot right good—
Some sanctuary by beauty graced.
Then on the cheek the Rose he traced,
The Lily on the bosom placed
    Of English maidenhood.

WASTE PLACES.

IF in the garden, nursed with care,
   Rich flowers, all flaunting, grow;
Yet oft on spots called WASTE and BARE
   The rarest wildlings blow!

THE BROOKLET:

There is sanctity about a clear brook or a mountain well.

I SING of a crystal brooklet,
　That shimmers in the sun ;
Its bed is soft with vernal green,
　Till its little course is run.

It whispers from a lakelet,
　That mirrors wooded hills ;
Its shore is bowers of fragrant flowers,
　Whose beauty ever thrills.

And the brooklet's crystal twinkles,
　So fresh, and sweet, and cool ;
And the flowers press its banks to dress,
　Or nod in each limpid pool.

So I rest by the bonnie brooklet,
　When the autumn leaves are sere,
And the Bramble's eye—like a maiden's, shy—
　Doth glance on its bosom, clear.

Dear image of my childhood,
　When my heart was pure like thee ;
Ere the muddy strife of manhood's life
　Was merged in an unknown sea !

O, thing of grace ! in thy angel face,
　I read of the golden shore ;
Of its crystal sea, and its harmony,
　When the toils of earth are o'er !

MAY.

Now virgin May herself arrays
To meet the happy Poet's gaze.
Around her brow how sweetly plays
    The creamy Thorn,
While blue the Hyacinthine haze
    Her skirts adorn.

About her breasts the Broom doth blow,—
With thousand tints her garments glow,
With stars her golden hair doth flow
    In clusters sweet;
While cascades all their gems do throw
    About her feet!

How pleasing 'tis at noon to lie
Amid the Hyacinthine dye
That forms a blue ambrosial sky
    All through the copse,
While bright the happy moments fly
    On new fledged hopes!

THE LIME TREE.

(*Tilia Europæa.*)

I SAW blithe Spring—whose nimble feet
    Were oft bepowdered with the snow—
With Catkins hang the Birks so sweet,
    And robe in white the leafless Sloe,

And breathe his breath across the trees,
    Hang bee and blossom from the Plane,
While wafted on the soft'ning breeze
    The Throstle poured his sweetest strain.

When Spring had decked the woods all fair
    And from the Ash her wine buds pressed,
He vanished through the Summer air,
    And warmer days the Lime hath dress'd.

The Lime—the last of forest trees
    To part with all her honeyed store—
When corn is yellow calls the bees
    To roam at will her treasures o'er.

Yes, thou, sweet Linden, art a type
    Of wealthy men, who, late to give,
Give lavishly—their purpose ripe—
    Fling gifts that make their memory live.

Stand 'neath the Linden's minster shade,
    And breathe the incense of her air,
And let her noonday psalm pervade
    Thy inner self—and worship there !

TO THE COMMON WOUNDWORT.*

(*Stachys Sylvatica*).

I would advise my readers to beware lest they in a solitary ramble
with a friend should mistake this plant for Wild Mint (which it closely
resembles, *in appearance only*), and cull a sprig of it for presentation.

> FOUL Stachys! Woundwort!—that's thy name—
> Thou ne'er shalt set my muse aflame;
> But I'll rhyme something, all the same,
>   Though not in praise;
> I scarce dare drag thee into fame,
>   With thy bad ways.
>
> The Nettle's form thou dost assume:
> Her sting may cloud our face in gloom;
> Yet in the pot for her there's room,
>   'Mong Scottish kail,
> That makes the rosy faces bloom
>   Of bairnies hale.
>
> Stachys! A poet hath a nose,
> And thou art of its dreaded foes.
> By lonely glens, where'er he goes
>   To muse a while,
> He meets, like unforgotten woes,
>   Thy odour vile!

---

* The Nettle protects itself by its stings. The Woundwort, which
has a leaf exceedingly like that of the Nettle, wards off its enemies by
its offensive odour, like that General in ancient history who placed
the stink pots between his army and the pursuing foe.

If 'mong the flowers he happy stray
By burn, or brake, or sunny brae,
He's sure to tread thee in his way,
    O, Stachys dread !
But of thee he's no more to say—
    Thou'rt of the dead !

TO THE BLAEBERRY.

(BILBERRY OR WHORTLEBERRY.)

(*Vaccinium Europœa.*)

OFT hae I sang the wildling flowers
By heath an' hill an' woodland bowers—
By trouty burns an' ivied towers—
    In Spring an' Simmer ;
But though my muse on you aft glowers,
    It's aye been timmer !

Blaeberry—Gather roun' the Nine,
(Least I my rustic sang should tine),
An' dye wi' your sweet purple wine
    Their dewy lips,
That thou mayest hear hoo fair an' fine
    My measure trips !

Hoo sweet thou art in Lassie Spring
When ower your bells the Lavrocks sing,
And early bees are on the wing
    Amang their blushes ;
In crimson beauty sweet they hing
    Mang heather bushes.

An', O, whan Simmer rules the sky,
An' Flora's fragrant train sweeps bye ;
Hoo pleasing 'neath the pines to lie
    An' gust the gab
Wi' thy sweet berries—Tyrian dye
    Is in ilk blab !

THE BURNET ROSE.

This lowly haunter of the sand dunes, though never rising more than a few inches above the ground—its blossoms often touching their mother earth—is the sweetest scented of all the rose family.

O SWEET is the breath of the summer sea,
As it stealeth at noon o'er the clover'd lea ;
But sweeter than all, beyond compare—
Tho' its stem be thorny, its garden bare ;
Tho' on sandy dunes it humbly grows—
Is the loved and the lowly Burnet Rose.

This lowly flower, with her petals pale,
That wafteth her incense on the gale,
Tho' her bed be the earth, yet her odour sweet
The airy angels of morning greet,
As they shake the dew from their bless'd repose,
And kiss the lips of the Burnet Rose.

O, dreamy as music steals in glens,
Cooler than springs in bosky dens,
Sweet as the kiss that Love first drew,
Clearer than flights ever poet flew,
Is the witching spirit that tender blows
In the balmy breath of the Burnet Rose.

TO THE WALLFLOWER.

(*Cheiranthus Cheiri.*)

This flower grows in profusion on the Castle Rock, Edinburgh.

WHEN first I spied thee as a wildling, thou
Wast goldening the giddy rocks beneath
Edina's ancient fort, there wafting far
Thy rarest odour to the heedless wind,
Far up beyond the hand that fain would pluck
Thy bronzèd beauty, like a maiden coy
In some high palace, where Love lingers near,
Yet may not climb, or, daring, fears a fall.
But in the garden thou art Spring's delight,
When apple trees shower blossoms at thy feet,
And music raineth from the larky sky.
Sweet-breath'd brunette, thou art beloved by all !—
How soft thy cheek—thy beauty is as Youth !
Thy perfume is thine own : no rival bloom
Breathes thy sweet breath. When thou art near to bless
Thou wakest in my mind all pure delights,
And lead'st me captive in fair Flora's train.

TO THE COMMON SPEEDWELL.

(*Veronica Officinalis.*)

WHERE'ER I meet thee, up doth Fancy fly
In thoughts celestial—Image of the sky !
About thee shining, starry Daisies sing,
And from their hosts the joyous Lark doth spring ;
While Dandelion suns around thee blaze,
And Lady's-smock, dipped in Aurora's rays,
Wafts o'er thy petals blue, an odour, sweet
As dawn of love—let me thy beauty greet
With my faint song, dear, tender, fragile flow'r
That from the azure vault once drew thy dow'r !
When mine do gaze upon thy laughing eyes,
I have one wish—to pluck thee as a prize ;
But that I know thine eyes were never made
To mock the sky, save from the dewy glade :
Even as a modest maiden, reared amid
The pieties of Nature, that lie hid
In forms like thine, blooms fairest where she grows,
And of deceitful Art but little knows !
Thou art a jewel on the brow of May,
That, robed in scented garments, wings her way !

Emblem of Friendship—rarest gem of blue—
From me thou ever hast affection true !

THE MISTLETOE.

(*Viscum Album.*)

A RHYME FOR THE CHILDREN.

Come, gather round, my chubby ones,—
The winter's come, you know ;
I'll tell you of that wondrous plant
The sacred Mistletoe !
I'm sure you all have oft admired
Its berries—just like pearls ;
And, 'neath its boughs you've often seen
The boys kiss the girls !

Well ! Do you know, this plant so queer
Ne'er grew in any soil :
"How can that be ?" I hear you say,
Yet, listen ; and don't smile :—
It's just a wretched parasite,
And grows on orchard trees :
Yes, just like folks called " hangers-on,"
Or "spongers" if you please !

When once its pretty pearls are ripe,
The Throstles from the wood
Come hopping o'er its branches green
And pick the pearls for food :
And oft their viscous, gluey blobs
Stick to their feet and wings,
And then they fly to other trees
And rub them off—poor things !—

And thus the birds are gardeners too—
Unconsciously they sow
Upon the apple, oak, or beech
The sacred Mistletoe !

And long before the Romans came
To fight our savage sires,
The Druids burned the Mistletoe
Amid their festal fires.
And when stern Winter swept his blasts
Across their fields so poor ;
To still his rage, the Mistletoe
Was hung above each door :
They counted it a sacred thing,
And offered it to Baal
Their cruel God in sacrifice :—
That is an ancient tale !

But now the Mistletoe adorns
The feast we hold more dear—
The birth of Him who speaketh peace
In every sinner's ear.

LINES,

SUGGESTED BY A VISIT TO THE CELEBRATED ROSE GARDEN OF MR. THOMAS TODD AT BROOMHOUSE.

Mr. Todd (fruit merchant, Gallowgate, Glasgow) has one of the best and largest collection of roses in the country ; and the astonishing thing is that nearly all of them are Dutch varieties —imported direct. His display is proof that Dutch roses can do splendidly in Scotland.

O, WAD ye like to see the Rose
Clad in the grace Perfection throws ;
Or wad ye feast for ance yer nose
     On odours sweet ?
Then aff tae Broomhouse !   There she blows
     Wi' charms replete !

For me, I gat a braw surprise,
An' thocht me 'neath Italian skies
Or 'mang the glades o' Paradise
     In Tammie's yaird :
Roses o' every hue an' size
     Ma' glowerin' shared !

Roses in thoosans—red an' white,
Or streakéd like Aurora bright,
An' ithers in Carnation dight
     Wi' buff between—
A very garden o' delight
     For poets' een !

But what gart me ma' pow whiles claw,
Was hoo Tom Todd could name them a'—
Princes and lords, an' ladies braw,
      Poets and sages,
Great names at hame an' far awa'
      Wad filled sax pages !

Frae Holland, tae, I'm tauld by Tam,
This galaxy o' queens a' cam',
Prize-catchers a' at Amsterdam
      An' ither toons ;
An' mony a Dutchman's drained his dram
      To grace their croons.

My blessin' on thee, Tammas Todd,
Sin' I amang yer roses trod !
A sicht o' them micht ease the load
      O' warldly care,
An' send us whistling doon Life's road
      A livelier air !

THE WILD HYACINTH.

(*Agraphis Nutans.*)

FLEECY and blue is the sky o'erhead :
　　　But I pensive lie
　　　On a living sky—
For the blue Agraphis is my bed !

And wide as my raptured eye can reach
　　　Are its scented bells :
　　　And their music tells
Of our Father's love : and I list their speech.

See ! The children's arms can bear no more
　　　Of the breathing blue !—
　　　And with pleasures true
They are turning their treasures o'er and o'er !

I could lie all day 'mong the odour sweet,
　　　And for ever gaze
　　　On the steady haze
Of the Hyacinths about my feet—

While the Stichwort's stars through the blue smoke
　　shine,
　　　And the Lychnis red
　　　Hath its glory spread,
And the Broom laughs out from its golden mine !

THE POET'S GARDEN.

"Where lies the Poet's garden ?   Where ?
  For I would breathe its balmy air !
What fairest flowers !   What fruity boughs !
  What garlands for his lady's brows !
Where is the Poet's garden ?   Say :
  That in it I may wandering stray ? "—
Thou canst not see his clustering vine
  If thou hast not the vision Fine !

His garden doth unmeasured lie :
  Its walls, the hills ; its roof, the sky ;
Its fountains fall 'mong fleecy flocks ;—
  Its statues are the mossy rocks ;—
Its music wild, the winds and waves—
  Or where the tumbling torrent raves !
But its full chords thou canst not hear,
  If thou hast not the Gifted Ear !

Among its never-ending walks
  With Fancy still the Poet talks :
Its vistas stretch remote and far,
  And, rising, kiss the morning star !
Ten thousand lights illume his way,
  And make it one unending day.
But canst thou see how bright they shine
  If thou hast not the Vision Fine ?

The Poet's garden is the world,
Or where in pomp the clouds are hurled
In wreaths of glory, high upborne !—
Sun, moon, and stars ; the dewy morn,
The lark's loud lay ; all fragrant flowers,
The fleecy winter—summer's showers ;
All blend harmonious in his verse—
His garden is the UNIVERSE !

TO THE FOLKSGLOVES IN CALDER GLEN.

JUNE, 1895.

I have never seen this stately flower so plentiful nor in such magni-
ficence as in the upper portion of Calder Glen, near Lochwinnoch.

WHY should I long to roam afar
  Amid the tropics' floral wealth,
When your gay forms adorn each scar
  Of Scotia's glens—the haunts of health ?
Yea, to my fancy, it appears
Ye are Queen Flora's Grenadiers !

Queen Flora holdeth high levee
  Beside the crystal waters cool ;
Her minstrels sing from every tree,
  And fragrant flowers bend dutiful—
Well guarded by your awful spears,
Imperial, purpled Grenadiers !

Fair queenly flowers, rare perfumed o'er,
  Or pensive as young maidens shy,
All sweetly deck the garnished floor
  Where Violets and Speedwells vie
In beauty ! yet no fair one fears—
Guarded by you—gay Grenadiers !

And Calder Glen keeps holiday
  While your proud forms like sentries stand :
With bounding heart I upward stray ;
  Nor would I lift a ruthless hand
To break the glory of your spears—
For ye are Flora's Grenadiers !

THE BRAMBLE IN OCTOBER.

THE flora of the year is past—
    Adown the lanes I ramble,
The faded leaves are falling fast,
    Yet jetty hangs the Bramble.

Its blossoms still are silken white,
    And black, and red, and green,
Its berries dangle with delight—
    Fit jewels for a queen.

The Hazel all its nuts hath shed
    In many a cozy nook,
And all the flowers have gone to bed
    And closed is Flora's book.

But still the Bramble's raven eye
    Doth glance beneath the bracken,
And many a bank doth beautify
    By every flower forsaken.

ON THE SAME IN NOVEMBER.

THE loveliest, the last and best—
    The glory of the year—
Behold ! the hoary frost hath press'd
    And dimm'd its eye so clear.

Now, woeful wan it hangs its head
  Beneath November's blast,
The beauty of the year hath sped—
  The snow is falling fast.

Yet, when September's suns have shone,
  As by the woods I ramble,
Mine eyes may meet when musing lone
  The glances of the Bramble.

TO THE BRAMBLE.

OCTOBER sets thy leaves ablaze,
And warms my muse to sing thy praise,
Dear Bramble ! Oft my doublet thin
Thou used to rive, when round the linn
I scrambled for thy clusters ripe,
Black glancing 'neath the Haw and Hip
Like maidens' eyes. And truth to tell,
In manhood's years thou fling'st a spell
To charm my eyes or please my taste,
While Autumn doth to Winter haste !

Thy silken blossoms white and gay
Seem pretty children out to play ;
Thy berries green, their days at school,
Soured with each task of book and rule ;
Till larger grown, thy berries show
Their ruddy bloom, like healthy glow

Of manhood, spurred by Love's warm flame
On to the goal of wealth or fame,
Till like thy berries black, it wage
No more the strife—in ripe old age.

Tho' Life 'mid cruel prickles grow—
Like thee it may soft blossoms throw ;
And, if with kindly Faith as root,
Leave to old Earth some precious fruit.
Yea, what a lesson thou dost preach
When dangling high—beyond my reach—
Thy envied blobs !   Thus beauty rare
And things most lovely, sweet and fair—
To call these mine, I must, alas,
Through pain and toil and suffering pass,
Ah ! He who brought the soul its bread,
Had crown of thorns about His head !

Thanks, lowly Bramble of the brake,
From you bless'd lessons oft I take !

TO THE DEVIL'S-BIT SCABIOUS.*

(*Scabiosa Succiso.*)

MY grandsires gazed with curious eyes
On you, my pretty mountain prize !
Perhaps in fear their thoughts would run
Unbidden to the Evil One
That haunted tree, and vale, and hill,
And farm, and fen, and stream, and mill,
And on thy rhizome set his seal,
Lest thy rich beauty might reveal
To passer's gaze the hand Divine
That made thy dome in purple shine !

With brighter vision I behold
Thy matchless hive of bloom unfold,
Thy arching form, to Fancy's eye
May seem an image of the sky
Without a cloud !
. . . . . . But to the bee
Thou art a honied treasury.
Mayhap the fairies name thy towers—
"Rare bouquets for the queen of flowers."

When snows lie deep, and winter's spear
Lays low the pageant of the year,
I'll miss thee by the moorland burn,
And, longing, sigh for thy return !

---

* The Rhizome of this plant is abrupt, as if cut off with a blunt instrument. The ancients of course believed that the Devil bit it off, to prevent it being used as a medicine. The flower head is not unlike a bee-hive.

TO THE FOXGLOVE (POISONOUS).

(Digitalis Purpurea.)

GREAT guardian of the summer flowers ;
   Stern watcher of the dappled fields !
Thou tall Dragoon by Flora's bowers,
   A painful death thy sabre wields !
When I was small, I wondering stood,
   Approached thy regal form with fear :
Whene'er I met thee by some wood
   I scarce dared break thy crimsoned spear !

TO THE CORN MUSTARD OR CHARLOCK.

(*Sinapis Arvensis.*)

" THE farmer's pest," good people say,
As they behold thee make thy way
Across the greening fields in May,
    Sinapis.

Yet, gleaming o'er the earless field,
With ne'er a hedgerow for a shield,
Thou dost to me sweet pleasure yield—
    Sinapis.

How gladsome, on a sweet June morn,
To mark thy yellow light adorn
The glades of verdant tender corn—
    Sinapis.

And when the zephyr comes to greet
The flower-crowned spring with nimble feet,
I, ravished, catch thy odour sweet—
    Sinapis.

Or should a cloud its shadow flit
Across the field, thou'lt follow it
Like sunshine, or a poet's wit—
    Sinapis !

I meet thee in October mellow,
And note that thou hast ne'er a fellow
To match thee for thy coat of yellow—
    Sinapis !

On moor or fen thou wilt not grow,
But where men till and plant and mow
There I behold thy social glow—
                    Sinapis.

But tell it not to farmer Brown,
A poet holds thee in renown,
And deigns to sing thy yellow gown—
                    Sinapis !

NUTTING TIME.

October in scarlet and russet and grey
   Is hymning of Plenty and wine :
So, with hearts light as air, let us up and away
   Through the glen where the gay berries shine.

How calm is the morn ! In high treble the stream
   Is singing in rambling measure
Like a bard all enrapt that would catch on a theme
   In the mazes of Fancy and pleasure !

O, a-nutting we go ! Now the bloom's on the sloe ; *
   And the Guelder-rose clusters are gay
In glossy carnation ! How bright is the glow
   Of the Hip—fairy lamp of the day !

'Mong the Brackens so brown how the Brambles do
      glance
   As witching as Jenny's dark eyes
As she glides like a Grace through the hall in the dance
   And her heart still a coveted prize !

O, the joys of nutting ! The clusters hang high,
   But the crook brings the branches anear,
And the fringed involucre that shades the bold eye
   To our fingers and pockets is dear !

---

* The bloom of its fruit.

We strip the bold clusters and set the branch free,
　And deem we have all its nuts shaken ;
But others pop out 'neath the leaves, we can see,
　So we own we are somewhat mistaken.

So Nutters who follow may gather and glean,
　Though to us it may prove tantalizing :
On the fair tree of knowledge is fruit always seen,
　And to each generation enticing.

O, money can't buy the delights of the glen,
　Nor Poetry sing all its charms :
There's a solace and calm ne'er described by the pen
　When we're folded within Nature's arms !

THE CAMELLIA AND THE ROSE.

A MORAL.

In the language of flowers, the White Camellia is the symbol of "Perfected Loveliness," yet it lacks perfume ; the Rose has ever been dear to "The Ruling Passion."

BENEATH a crystal dome and shade—
   Safe sheltered from the blustering storm—
There bloomed, I ween, the loveliest maid
   That ever bore fair Flora's form !—
Her bosom might the snow-flake shame :
Camellia was her choral name.

Beside her grew a damask Rose—
   Her odour breathing all around :
To match this pair there never grows
   Such Form and Sweetness from the ground.
Perfection of all Beauties fair—
Perfection of all Perfumes rare !

The lovely fair Camellia spake,
   And thus the queen of flowers addressed :—
" Ah ! could I but thy fragrance take,
   Young Love had sure my petals pressed ;
Yet why, since he thy court adorns,
Must he be hedged about with thorns ? "

Then spake the flower of Love and Song :
   " I must be wooed, fair evergreen ;
Yet, bold must be the heart and strong
   That wins the blushes of a queen ;
And he who highest bliss would gain,
Must tread the thorny path of pain ! "

A nymph—whose brow the Lily shows,
   Her breasts full acorns in October—
Heard fair Camellia and the Rose,
   And bade them list to counsel sober :
Beauty and Perfume, heavenly pair,
Heard Poesy this truth declare :—

" Learn, maidens : God hath kindly given
   Some charm to every living thing :—
The Lark that, singing, soars to heaven,
   He plumeth not the Pheasant's wing ;
The Peacock draped in rainbow shades
Ne'er wakes to song the sleepy glades !

And thou, Camellia, to the eye,
   Hast ne'er a rival !   Why repine
If Perfume Nature thee deny ?
   Thy gay green dress hath ne'er a spine :
No cruel thorn upon thee grows—
So, live content beside the Rose ! "

TO THE MARSH MARIGOLD.

(Caltha Palustris.—Literally, the fire or lamp of the meadow.)

THOU sett'st the meadows all ablaze
    To welcome in the May ;
Where'er the crystal burnie strays
    I mark thy blossoms gay.
O, that I could thy charms unfold—
My cheery, gay Marsh Marigold !

Thy golden flame yet warms my breast,
    As in the Springs long fled,
When, searching for the wild bird's nest,
    I saw thy splendour spread
About the marsh like floral fire,
And still thou art my heart's desire !

The cuckoo-flower's gauzy dress
    Looks gayer in thy gleams ;
Thy gold—her lilac, sweet caress
    Beside the limpid streams.
Thou bringest joys manifold—
My winsome gay—Marsh Marigold !

TO THE HOLLY.

(*Ilex Aquifolium.*)

WHEN trees are hung with icy beads,
　Thy red and green shine brightest, Holly;
Gayest when Nature wears her weeds,
　And drapes herself in melancholy.

To meet thee by some giddy glen,
　Thy berries blushing 'mong the snow,
Thou seem'st a type of good old men
　Whose cheeks still wear their youthful glow,
With hearts aye young and evergreen
　Of healthy cheer devoid of folly—
Like thee, full beautiful, I ween,
　My sturdy, gleesome, gay, green Holly.

When Winter rolls his crispy car
　Across the bleak and barren plains,
I see arise a wondrous star,
　And hear far-off angelic strains.
For, lo ! the merry bells ring in
　The birthday of the "Meek and Lowly ; "
The world hath ceased its warring din ;
　And crowns His natal feast with Holly.

LEAVES, OR DECAY AND DEATH.

DECAY.

WHILE roaming pensive 'mong the silent woods,
When mellow Autumn drapes them in her gold
And russet robes, we feel a holy calm
Pervade us, as the tinted leaves fall soft
About our path, or glow with fruit-like hues
From Beech and Elm and sweeping Chestnut fair.
Beneath the mighty Painter's silent touch
How charming this Fruition and Decay :—
This peaceful filling of the kindly lap
Of Mother Earth, with past gifts beautified !
Yet say not this is Death.

DEATH.

      Go pace the woods
When Summer o'er them throws her favourite hue.
High roars the blast; and Air's dread ocean heaves
The green expanse, and flings a wrenched branch
Of foliage fair athwart your unsafe path :
Call *this* Destruction—Death ! Go scan that limb,
When Autumn's golden tresses sweep the ground,
And mark the haggard aspect of its leaves
Still clinging like dead infants to a breast
That holds no generous store. Then pause ! Reflect !

TO THE OX-EYE-DAISY.

(Chrysanthemum Leacanthemum.)

'TIS drowsy June : the Muse, tho' lazy,
Yet wakes to sing thee, Ox-eye-Daisy !
Thy handsome form hath silent power
When thy great eye begins to glower
From rosy banks and broomy braes—
Where'er the flower-adorer strays !

Thy modest sister of the lea—
At noon a rarest pearl is she ;
But when Aurora chafes the night,
Wee Daisy wears a ruby bright :
Yet darkest night nor nimbus sky
Can make thee ever close thine eye ;
But thy white beams for ever play
About thy disk—so bright and gay !

What cunning Compass drew each line
Wherein thy golden florets shine ?
What fairy fingers ere could space
Each nectar'd cup within its place !
And so in thy great eye I see
A very world of mystery !

TO THE COMMON PEARL-WORT.

(Sagina Procumbens.)

This is perhaps the smallest flowering plant in Britain ; its nodding capsule resembles a pearl.

LITTLE croucher by the wall,
  Hast thou never heard a song ?
Is it that thou wast so small ?
  Then the poets did thee wrong !

Thou art lowly—scarcely seen—
  Yet thou hold'st a pretty gem ;
For, above thy robe of green
  Nods a pearly diadem !

Were Humility my theme,
  Rare similitude wert thou ;
For there darts a heavenward beam
  From a jewel on her brow !

LINES

ON A POSIE OF PURPLE SWEET VIOLETS AND GOLDEN DAFFODILS.

Violet and Yellow are complementary colours.

IMPERIAL Purple, royal Gold,
　　Dame Nature's complementary hues,
Your beauty never groweth old ;
　　A sense of pleasure ye diffuse,　　　·
　　　　Like harmony amongst the hills,
　　　　Sweet Violets and Daffodils !

Philosophy I shall not ask
　　Why ye so winsome draw together ;
I only in your beauty bask,
　　As doth a lane in sunny weather ;
　　　　Till rapture all my being fills,
　　　　Wed Violets and Daffodils !

Thy glory, Daffodil's, thy dower ;
　　Thy breath, Viola, is thy charm ;
And I could wish that human power
　　With Beauty so went arm in arm;
　　　　'Twould change a thousand Mortal ills
　　　　To Violets and Daffodils !

TO THE PLANE TREE.

(Acer Pseudo-platanus.)

The language of the Plane is *Genius.*

As a fair, fresh fancy illumes his brain
    And brightens the poet's eye,
So spreadeth thy palmy leaves, O Plane,
    'Neath the fleecy April sky !

Like a Milton's muse is thy grandeur calm
    And thy massive dome of green ;
And when noon rides high 'tis a healing balm
    To rest 'neath thy ample screen !

'Mong thy nectared blossoms low hymn the bees
    Like a hallowed fane in prayer ;
While thy incense stirred by the sighing breeze
    Perfumeth the list'ning air !

Grand symbol thou of Genius—Power—
    And Beauty and Thought sublime ;
And I deem thee of Nature the wealthiest dower
    That blesseth our northern clime !

AUTUMN.

Now Nature dons her tawny gown,
   And to her rest doth creep :
She's laid aside her Summer crown,
   And sadly sinks to sleep.
Soft, pensive feelings now I own
   Within my bosom stray,
While wandering by the woodland lone
   That rings no Throstle's lay—
All hushed !—save that the Redbreast trills
   His tender, tearful song,
Responsive to the whispering rills :
   Might I his strain prolong,
I'd mourn the King-cups broken all,
   The blue-eyed Speedwell dead—
The Primrose by the waterfall,
   Her saffron beauty shed—
The Hyacinth's rare perfume lost
   (All save its memory dear),
The Foxgloves stately—of their host
   Snapped is each purpled spear.
Snow drifts of fragrant Hawthorn, they
   Have melted from my view ;
Of all the galaxy of May,
   Dimmed is each lovely hue !

And, grateful for the beauty thrown
   Each year to bless our eyes,
What mortal knows, when Autumn's blown,
   If Spring, in myriad dyes,

Again he'll see ?   Thus Autumn mild
  And pensive hath her speech
On swift decay to man and child :—
  Each fading flower doth preach !
Yea, this I know, that mother earth
  Shall mantled be in green—
That Nature yearly giveth birth
  To Beauty, that hath been
And still shall be ?   Mankind behold
  God's lovely pageant pass
Before their eyes, that soon grow old,
  Then slumber 'neath the grass.

TO THE WHITE BIRCH.

CALLED BY ARTISTS "THE LADY OF THE FOREST."

(Betula Alba.)

SWEET fragrant fountain of fair foliage !
I hail thy showering beauty, by the lake
That mirrors all thy grace upon its page
    Where all thy twinkling leaves soft-shimmering shake!
    Or let me call thee Lady of the Brake,
Where waving ferns adoring kiss thy feet,
    And Blackbirds all the glens to echoes wake
And vernal rains allure thy perfume sweet,
While round thee and afar with joy the flowerets meet.

Thy beauteous form, fair Birch, we often trace
    By cunning brush, and proudly call this Art ;
But who the waving witchery and grace,
    That wakes the latent music of the heart—
    Can ere to lifeless canvas once impart ?
Who paint thy perfume after genial showers,
    Or the soft sighings of thy leaves, that start
The sleeping memories of our childhood hours
When free from care as thou we culled our fairest
        flowers ?

TO THE FALLS OF FOYERS.
VISITED 8TH AUGUST, 1893.

FOYERS—thy foaming form still flings
　Her misty showers around the pine,
And gems with noontide dew the wings
　Of flowers that 'neath thy rainbow shine.
Here, where the umbrageous trees do twine
　Their roots around the rifted rock,
My spirit in thy roar doth join—
　The deep, hoarse thunder, and the shock
　That evermore do Silence mock.

This warring Cauldron !　Hewn by thee
　Ere yet, perchance, Man's wondrous eyes
Had gazed upon thy majesty
　With terror or divine surprise !
Still thou seem'st pouring from the skies—
　The battered boulders bide thy roar.
Thou hast a voice that never dies !
　Silence ne'er trod thy temple's floor,
　Where rolls thy anthem evermore !

Foyers—thou hast thy temple built,
　Here thou art Priest and Prayer and Praise.
I, Son of Care, on shadows spilt,
　To thee but faint my pæans raise ;
Yet, on thy glories I may gaze,
　And join the triumphs of thy thunder !
There was an eye* once pierced thy haze ;
　That orb was sure the home of wonder
　As it surveyed thy crystal splendour !

---

* Burns visited these falls.

THE POPPIES IN THE CORN.

It is a striking instance of the struggle for existence, that the scarlet
poppy is found in greatest profusion amongst corn or wheat, where its
blossoms appear all the brighter in contrast to the green of the cereals
--green and scarlet being complementary colours.

POPPIES, Poppies, all the way,—
To right or left, where'er I stray:
Nor flirting high, nor all forlorn,
But flaunting 'mong the vernal corn !
Upon a rustic gate I lean,
To quaff the fragrance of the bean ;
But through the corn my charméd eye
Doth catch the Poppy's scarlet dye.

I ask myself this question plain—
" What doth this flower amongst the grain ?
Why are its fickle petals rife
Beside the ancient staff of life ?
Its rosy hues—though fading fast—
Flame brighter by the green contrast."

Ah, types of vain extravagance !
Amid the sturdy grain you dance
But one short day.   Then wan and weak—
The crimson faded from each cheek,
Your glory spent like setting sun—
What praise or blessings have ye won ?
While, marching to some merry strain,
Men carry home the golden grain.

And there are human Poppies, sure—
We call them rich ; but they are poor !
Their motto " Take," but never " Give ; "
For pomp and show they only live.
Corn *Labour* dyes their garments gay,
Yet fleet and fitful is their day.

TO THE WALLACE OAK IN THE FOUNTAIN GARDENS, PAISLEY.*

My puir wee stunted, crouchin' thing ;
Thy form wad ne'er mak' bardies sing :
Tho' hallowed memories round thee cling—
  My heart is sair
To see ye show, in leafy Spring,
  Yer stumpies bare !

Are ye a son o' that bauld Aik
Aft screened the Knight gart England quake,
And drew his sword for Scotland's sake
  An' Libertie ?
Ye'r liker some decrepit rake
  New aff the spree !

Maybe thou say'st wi' crecklin' face,
That Scotia's shortenin' her pace,
An' faggin' fast in Freedom's race,
  Wi' gowd weighed doon ?
Something like that I think I trace
  In thy wee froon.

Folk hint, puir thing, ye need protection
Frae knaves wa'd slit ye for dissection,
An' haun yer limbs roun' for inspection
  When stiff an' deid :—
Sic Antiquarian cursed infection
  Maun e'en tak' heid :

---

* Planted at the opening of these Gardens, and grown from an acorn
from the aged oak which grew at Elderslie—the birthplace of Wallace.
The hero oft hid from his enemies in its boughs.

For Seestu bodies mean to shield
Yer tawted tap wi' speary bield ;
An' whan sax hunner year are reeled
    By Spinner Time,
To some puir poet ye may yield
    A theme sublime !

THE BRAMBLES IN THE WHINS.

"We joy in tribulations also."—PAUL.

THE whins now cover all the path
  That led me merry home from school,
When my young heart, devoid of wrath,
  Knew little save the golden rule.
Now scarce I drag my tortured limbs
  O'er this rough tangled hill of thorn ;
My heart with fire enough up brims
  Might burn it ere to-morrow morn.
Lo ! here are brambles growing near,
  But not a ripe one can I see ;
For children's fingers have been here—
  That is as plain as well might be.
Yet, with my stick the whins I ope,
  And with my feet their prickles tread,
When, gladsome as the gleams of hope,
  Full many a cluster, black and red,
Of sheltered brambles, all unseen,
  Well hidden from the tiny hands.
I eat my fill of them, I ween,
  Nor grudge the gorse its well-earned lands.
Thus should the soul, from bitter sorrow,
Some sweet refreshment ever borrow !

THE POET TO THE NETTLE.

WHAT poet would thy praises sing,
   Thou vegetable adder ?
And for his lays receive thy sting,
   To make his muse the madder ?
The thought of thee new pain suggests
   Thou foe of every hand !
Thou'rt in the van of Flora's pests—
   'Gainst thee I take my stand !
I'll grip thee firm—and all thy kind
   That spurn at soft address,
Whose sting in every word we find,
   And in the feigned caress !
I hate thee, Nettle ! What's thy place
   In earth's economy ?
I care not I ne'er see thy face,
   Nor folks that act like thee !

THE NETTLE'S REPLY TO THE POET.

You ask me to define my place
   In earth's economy,
And why I've not the winning face
   Of gaudy flowers folks see ?
I'll try. I've fought for ages long
   The battle of existence,
In which some lose who are not strong,
   Some win by sheer resistance ;
Some flaunt gay colours to allure,
   And some the air perfume ;
While others—worse than me, I'm sure—
   (Like spiders in your room)
Set cruel snares to catch a fly ;
   Some send their youngest born
To prey on some beast passing by ;
   And some your fair earth scorn,
And thrive well on your fair fruit trees ;
   Some climb upon your walls,
Some set sweet meshes for the bees,
   And some, as evening falls,
By fragrance woo the silken moth—
   And all are in the fray,
The fight for Life, not one is loth ;
   And note now what I say :—
I woo the wind—but not in sport—
   I wear no gaudy hues,
And tender folks tread not my court—
   My company I choose.
The breeze tends well my offspring dear,
   And plants them far and wide,
I own I am a little queer—
   But note, there's more beside :—
In short, Philosophy can show it,
   There's room for *Nettle* and for *Poet !*

TO THE FRAGRANCE OF THE ROSE.

AH, Rose! had'st thou but Beauty's charms
 Thou ne'er had been the poet's flower :
Extended on thy thorny arms
 Thou had'st not wielded sovereign power ;
Thy perfume is the royal spell
So is the love of Isabel.

Thy redolence,' bewitching queen,
 Doth haunt me all the summer days
Like incense from a world unseen,
 Where Innocence for ever strays ;
O, lave me in thy soothing spell,
That I may win fair Isabel.

Through all my being sweetly float
 Like music from a distant choir :
When thou art near, on love I dote,
 My heart is tuned to pure desire ;
Thou art a draught from God's deep well—
Thou art like Love and Isabel.

TO THE DEADLY NIGHTSHADE (No. 1).
(*Atropa Belladona.*)

The fruit of this rare but highly poisonous plant is lovely, and may fitly be compared to the dark eyes of women.

I GAZE upon thee as I might
On galaxy of dark Italian queens—
In some high hall around the festive board
Dealing destruction 'mong enamoured knights.
Can death lurk in those glorious glittering orbs
That glance at me from out the russet leaves ?
As witching to the untutored schoolboy's hand
As those fierce glances from old Nila's banks
That changed a warrior to a feeble child !
The Siren on the rock methinks thou art.
The poor deluded swain whom wanton eyes
Hath driven to despair, in thee may find
The soporific—Death.   And jealousy
Will close her sideling eyes at thy command !
The meanest weed that grows on rubbish heaps
Is dearer far to me than thou—proud queen !
And underneath a plain yet modest form
May beat the truest heart ; and Virtue rare
Abide for aye, where ne'er a glance betrays !

ATROPA BELLADONNA (No. 2).

ROBED in her Autumn dress of brown and sere,
The dark-eyed Belladonna glanced at me
With her wild wondrous eyes so clear :
And, charm'd, I thought can aught more glorious be ?
When old Experience passing by that way
Said, " Amorous youth, let not thy bosom swell ;
Love lurks not in those orbs, nor cheerful day :—
Behind them croucheth Death and deepest hell ! "

M

TO THE TUFTED VETCH CLIMBING OVER A HAWTHORN HEDGE.

(*Vicia Cracca.*)

HERE in the flower-clad lane, by hedgerows lined,
　I drink thy sunset beauty, climbing bright
Above the hawthorn's tops ; thy trusses twined
　Amid its lovely wreaths of fragrant white.

Imperial climber ! To thy flowery throne,
　Arrayed in purple, thou hast fought thy way
From lowly birth, thro' tortuous ways, alone,
　Till crowned at last thou gladdenst the day.

High up beyond the yearning children's hands,
　Thy blossoms catch the bee's quick anxious eye :
I mark her now, in robe of golden bands,
　In rapture hum amid thy Tyrian dye !

The Mayflower loads the breeze with odours sweet :
　She fades before the coming of the queen—
The love-fraught Rose—and pale about her feet ;
　But, in thy royal robes, thou at her court art seen !

MUSINGS AT PORTRUSH AND GIANT'S CAUSEWAY.

11TH AUGUST, 1892.

GREAT Ocean! Thy loud pulse for ever beats;
　I nurse new raptures by thy sounding shore.
A mortal here thy curling tresses greets,
　　And fain would sing a cadence to thy roar,
　　Which through thy caves doth echo evermore.
Thine eye shall never dim through ages vast,
　Eternal youth reigns in thy bosom's core.
Thy vigour riseth with the rising blast,
And thou art still the same when untold years have
　　passed.

Here Pluto's fires have burst in lava'd storms,
　　Leaving strange records of their vanquished rage
In sculptured columns, whose mysterious forms
　　Are wondrous pictures on great Nature's page;
　　And youngling science doth her powers engage
To read the records of the riven rocks:
　　While thou, dread ocean, ceaseless war doth wage
Against the reeling land with thunder shocks;
And even as she reads thy blinding fury mocks.

Great Rarifier of Air's ocean! Thou
　　That bearest healing in thy briny breath
To sickly man, and placest on his brow
　　　The bloom of health where stole the hand of Death.
　　　(" Sweet purifier," foul Corruption saith.)
Here 'mong the bee-toss'd bells and fragrant thyme,
　　The silken burnet rose and purple heath,
I list the hissing of thy salty rime,
And feel my being tuned to Nature's ceaseless chime.

A WILD FLOWER ALPHABET.

A—the Anemone, Spring doth unfold ;
B—is the Broom, with her tassels of gold.
C—Celandine, sung by Wordsworth the bard.
D—is the Daisy, the sun of the sward.
E—Eglantine, to the poets aye dear.
F—is the Folksglove—a bold Grenadier.
G—is the Gorse, making bird-nesters quail—
H—hoary Hawthorn, perfuming the gale.
I—is the Iris, by streams we must seek.
J—Jack-by-the-Hedge, with his breath like a leek.
K—is the Knapweed that crimsons the brake—
L—is the Lily, white nymph of the lake.
M—is the Melilot, fragrant when dry.
N—None-so-pretty, and well named, say I.
O—gives the Orchids—a statesman knows well.
P—is the Primrose, the moon of the dell.
Q—Queen-of-the-Meadow, sweet scenting the morn.
R—is the Rose : O, if minus her thorn !
S—is the Speedwell—she mocks the blue sky.
T—is the Thistle, that says " I defy ! "
U—Umbelliferous flowers—mostly white.
V—brings us Violets, breathing delight.
W—Woodbine, beloved for her breath.
X—names no flower—as a poet here saith.
Y—stands for Yarrow, a flower and a stream.
Z—is the Zephyr that round them doth dream ;
&—now, gentle reader, here endeth my theme.

A WILD FRUIT ALPHABET.

A—is the Acorn—aye filling his pipe.
B—is the Bramble, how tempting when ripe !
C—is the Cranberry, loves mossy fens.
D—is the Dewberry, haunter of glens.
E—Elderberries, that make a rich wine.
F—is the Filbert—a hazel-nut fine.
G—is the Gean, the grandma of the Cherry.
H—the Hagberry—'tis a Drupe, not a Berry.
I—Ivy berries, as black as a crow.
J—stands for Junipers—gin tipplers know.
K—the Knowtberries, 'mong bogs on the hill.
L—Lords and Ladies, that blackbirds won't kill.
M—is the Mountain Ash, yclept the Row'n.
N—Nightshade berries, in scarlet, green, brown.
O—Nature's Orchard—so dear to her child.
P—is the Plum, which we often find wild.
Q—is a Quart we may eat in the glen
R—of the Rasps, in some cool flowery den.
S—shows the Strawberries we ramblers prize.
T—is the Tutsan, like maiden's black eyes.
U—Upright-bramble—of deep crimson dye.
V—gives the Vetches we eat till we're dry.
W—Whorlly—the King of the Hips.
Y—scarlet Yews—that must ne'er cross our lips.
Z—is the zest that I hope you possess.
&—away o'er the moors for the wild fruits we'll
    press !

HAIRBELLS.

(Campanula Rotundifolia.)

By the flowery mountain path—
By the torrent's foaming wrath—
Far among the humming heather--
There the blue bells chime together.
On the rugged quarry's face
There they dangle with a grace,
Makes a poet's heart to leap
As the zephyrs round them sweep.

On their airy fairy stems
They hang like skiey gems—
Ever nodding in the breeze—
Ever bending to the bees.

Sweet azure bells—were ye
Once baptiséd in the sea,
Or, did ye to beauty wake
From the blue of Alpine lake ?
What are ye ever chiming—
To the poet ever rhyming ?
Ye make music in his heart
And his eye with fancy start,
As ye dangle and keep swinging,
On his full emotions ringing :
And how quick his spirit tells
All the music of your bells !

Hairbells—so blue ! so fair !—
Ye are living forms of air ;
And to Faith's discerning eyes
Ye are Angels from the skies.
And, in Winter, when you're missing,
And the sleety showers are hissing,
Wee loving fingers and blue eyes
Are gathering you in Paradise.

TO THE FIELD MUSHROOM.

(*Agaricus Campestris.*)

LET folks wha need to gang to schule
Despise thee—ca' thee "puddock's stool,"
An' maybe say the bard's a fule
    That rhymes o' thee :—
Thy silken ba' and salmon gill
    Are dear to me !

Thou art a rover o' the field,
Nae bush nor bracken asks't for bield,
Nor big'st thy beauty 'neath the shield
    O' craggy glen :
When seekin' thee I've never reeled
    Wi' headlong sten.

But 'mang the bleatin' o' the ewe,
An' rowtin' o' some cottar's coo,
Aft hae I marked wi' rapture new
    Thy silvery dome
O'erarching Beauty that ne'er grew
    In Greece or Rome.

Just when the corn begins to yellow
Thy pinky flesh grows sweet an' mellow ;
'Mang drippin' thou hast ne'er a fellow
    I' the skirlin' pan :
Aneath thy snaw-white umbrella
    There's feastin' gran' !

But when thou pour'st thy sauted bluid*
Thou mak'st a brander'd steak fu' guid :
Ye'll mak' a drouth's wan cheek grow red—
    His head to think,
An' whiskied stomachs fit for food
    E'en in a blink.

I've kent me whyles when far frae hame
Flower huntin'—wi' a hungry wame,
Gey prood to spy thy snawy kaim
    Like manna spread :
Far sweeter thou wert then than game
    On hauvers fed !

Sae, thou canst please the gab an' e'e—
A thing o' rare utility—
A very treasure unto me—
    Tho' short, fu' sweet ;
Thou an' the gourd micht preachers be
    On a' things fleet.

---

* Ketchup.

TO BUTTERFLIES.

Composed in the Dranse Valley, Switzerland.

YE silent seraphs, circling Flora's throne ;
  Ye flitting flowers of air, that sip delight
  From earth's sweet stars ere heaven's gems grow
    bright !
Like wreck of rainbows o'er the meadows blown,
Or gay Imagination wandering lone
  Through untrod realms—so is your happy flight
  Among the perfumed fields, which ye have dight
With beauty manifold—that soon is gone.
Ye silent wooers of the wishing flowers
  That, blushing, lure you to their honeyed halls,—
Dance out your golden day, and steal its hours,
  Till o'er you, as o'er men, Death's slumber falls :
Till Spring shall blow " Resurgum " o'er the lea,
And name you types of Immortality !

TO THE COMMON SUNDEW.

(*Drosera Rotundifolia.*)

This plant, which grows in wet boggy places, depends chiefly for its sustenance on the blood of little insects, which it captures by exposing on the leaves what looks to the silly fly drops of dew, but which are only blobs of transparent, viscid matter. When the insect alights the tentacles close round it and strangle the victim.

THE spider watching by his snare,
Weel hid, at noon, amang the air—
The brindled Tiger in his lair
    Wi' burnin' e'en—
Ne'er matched thee, Sundew, deadly, fair—
    Deception's queen !

When simmer shines, wi' ne'er a shoor,
Then is the day o' thy great power ;
Amang the moss ayont the moor
    Thou feastest fine,
An' mony a midge thou dost allure
    Its life to tine !

Aye ! Wha would think your rosy bed,
Wi' skinklin' jewels a' o'erspread
Is nocht else than a butcher's shed
    Or slaughter cairn :
An' thou thy victims ne'er hast bled
    Wi' steel or airn !

Wee, glaiket midge—that isna dew
Yer gaun to sip—I'll tell ye true
Thae di'monds a' are made o' glue,
  Then, O, beware,
Or else thy flirtin' thou shalt rue
  In sorrow sair !

O, artless maid ! This flower to thee
Doth point a lesson ; cans't thou see ?
Beware of Wealth's wild witchery—
  Th' *unreal* shun ;
The lowly cot a heaven may be—
  The palace none !

TO THE REED-MACE.

(*Typha Latifolia.*)

This stately plant is to be found on Loch Libo. It is erroneously called the bull-rush in many parts of the country, but it belongs to quite a different order from the rushes. Its aggregate spike of florets —forming a dense black mass—is not unlike a grenadier's bonnet ; the leaves resemble long sabres.

TYPHA ! thy glittering sabres shake
  Beneath the glancing of the sun
About the shallows of the lake,
    Like spoils of war by Flora won ;
      Or did she steal thy form from Mars
      While nursing him from's weary wars ?

Or did she send the armoured god—
  When first he'd form his sanguine blade—
Thy deft design, two-edged and broad,
  For Vulcan in the lurid shade ?
    Tell me thy warlike evolution—
    Did Flora dread some revolution ?

When first I saw thy waving spears,
  And sable sentries sullen stand
Round Libo's lake like grenadiers—
  I deemed it then a vision grand :
    And every year it pleaseth me
    Such regal forms again to see !

Typha !—go guard the lilies hoar,
  That lean on Libo's bosom fair ;
While o'er her woods the lark doth soar,
  And Flora's breath holds all the air,
    And o'er the sleeping watery plain
    The wild duck waves his widening train !

TO THE OX-EYE-DAISY.

(*Chrysanthemum Leucanthemum.*)

The following verses were written at the request of a friend, who, having read a former poem to the above flower, asked for another in " braid Scots."

Fu' blythe an' bonnie 'mang the sward—
Tho' maist folks pay ye sma' regard,
Or maybe ca' ye names sae hard,
  As big horse gowan—
Thou art the pride o' ilka bard
  That sees thee growin'.

In fragrant June, hoo pleased I stray
'Mang fields o' clover-dappled hay,
Whar purple vetch and lotus play,
  An' sweetly blend,
An' 'neath thy queenly blossoms gay,
  Adoring bend.

But, ah ! the whetted scythe—alas !—
To-morrow mows thee wi' the grass,
An' steals the gowd thou didst amass
  To gladden me ;
For Death's cauld, clammy haun' shall pass,
  An' close thy e'e.

But whar the roarin' engine clanks,
An' o'er the iron railway spanks,
Hoo bonnilie the fleetin' banks
  Thou dost adorn ;
There mony a ane thy beauty thanks,
  By blade ne'er shorn.

My Ox-eye Daisy, thour't a treasure ;
Whare'er we meet thou gi'est me pleasure ;
An' I could laud thee withoot measure—
    Chrysanthemum ;
Sae, whan my muse again has leisure,
    Thy praise she'll hum.

TO THE BROOM.

Tassell'd skirt of the maiden May ;
   Golden robe of the lady June !
Splendour of vale, and bank, and brae,
   Childhood's fancy, the poet's tune.
Lighting the wold with gladsome gleams,
Fringing with gold the silvery streams !

When the hyacinth is thine azure sky,
   Thou art as a cloud by the sunset press'd ;
With the violet shedding a purple dye,
   And the campion crimsoning all its crest :
O, the heart it knoweth nor care, nor gloom,
When the eyes do gaze on the golden broom !

TO THE COMMON COW-PARSNIP.

(*Heracleum Spohndylium.*)

WHEN Orrey did first define
How round the sun the planets shine ;
Methinks he studied long and humble
The symmetry of thy broad umbel—
Reared on its tubed peduncle strong—
A crown of stars for poet's song !

Thou art a mystery despised
By pampered folk ; yet richly prized
By men who have the " Inner eye,"
And in thy host of flowers descry
The Law of laws that blushed the Rose
And fixed the Oak in broad repose !

The tiny forms that round thee hum,
With rapture to thy banquet come ;
And there, when all thy silver's spread,
Are with thy sweetest dainties fed ;
And unseen fairies all the night
Sit round thy board with rare delight !

The Foxglove and the Lychnis gay
Salute me in the lanes each day ;
Though I admire their gaudy hues,
To turn to thee I'll ne'er refuse ;
But see in all that springs from earth
The Father of each wondrous birth !

N

TO THE IVY-LEAVED TOADFLAX.

(*Linaria Cymbalaria.*)

LINARIA CYMBALARIA !—
　There's music in thy name ;
But fringing this old castle wall
　Thou set'st my muse aflame !
How gracefully thy tresses wave
　Above the Ivy green—
Thine own, rare mimic of *his* robe,
　With jewels set, I ween,
Fit to adorn the fairest brow
　That strikes a poet's eye !
I marvel why dame Nature chose
　Such place for flower to die—
This haunted ruin old and grey !
　Perhaps she wished to teach
The human gazer lessons rare ;
　Mayhap to him she'd preach
That modesty still lives apart
　Nor courts the common gaze :
That Genius oft in garret grows—
　There blooms and ends its days !

TO THE HONEYSUCKLE OR WOODBINE.

LADS and lasses love the gloaming,
   Nature then the heart doth move ;
Poets then go forth a-roaming,
   Trysting with the Nine they love :
And, Woodbine, thy odour's sweetest
   When the star-rimmed cloudlets glow ;
Then the Sphynx-Moth,* thirsty, seeketh
   Where thy wells of honey flow.

Honeysuckle, honeysuckle !
   I feel young when clasping thee !
Down the lane wee bairnies buckle—
   Dancing "Innocence" and "Glee !"
Crystal burnies—birds a-singing—
   Balmy odours—thornless bower—
Loving whispers—hearts a-glowing—
   These thy dowry, maiden flower !

* Said to be the only moth that can fertilize this flower.

TO THE COMMON HEATHER.

(*Calluna Vulgaris.*)

My heart beats ever to a livelier tune,
When o'er the Grampians, like a vesture, hangs
Thy purple glow—bright Heather.   Summer's sun
Oft bathes the western hills in dolphin dyes
And glories evanescent; but thou sham'st
With thy abiding hue—thro' August days—
His setting splendours and his rising charms.
Thou art a thing of Liberty, and rid'st
On lofty Bens and giddy scars sublime,
Where bounds the stag with branching head erect,
And nostrils, farther piercing than the eye
Auxiliary of man his deadly foe.
Beneath thy shade protective clucks the Grouse ;
And 'mong thy bells the bee ecstatic reels,
Its one sole care the hive ; and little recks
It bears about thy fertilizing gold
From flower to flower 'mong all thy nodding sprays.
Thy sweet imperial charms dispel all care ;
And, walking in thy beauty all day long,
My blood steals half thy bloom, and floods my cheek.
After soft sunny showers, how delicate
The odour of thy breath—that wakens dreams
Of long lost Eden yet to be restored.

Now for the vase I'll pluck one lovely sprig
Of thy fair florets, that its tender blush
May bless me (till the weary winter wanes)
Like memories of a faithful friend, long gone !

A DREAM OF WILD FLOWER PERFUMES.

ONCE, through the boundless realm of sleep,
    Queen Flora took my hand
Thro' ferny dells, 'mong drooping bells—
    O'er hills—'neath mountains grand.

I said "O thou, divinely fair,
    What are those odours sweet—
Those unseen favours shed around,
    Man's wondrous sense to greet?"

She said—"God gave not flowers a speech,
    Nor winning charm of song;
But in their perfumes and their hues
    Love reigneth young and strong :—
By Robe and Breath they gently woo
    The rainbowed butterfly,
Or lure the deep-toned choiring bee
    As hymning he doth hie.
And so the endless web of Life
    Doth wrap this Earth so fair;
And all its secret threads inwove
    The Unseen's hand declare."

"Now woo the fragrance of the flowers,"
    She said, with beaming eyes,
"And tell me, with the voice of song,
    To which thou'lt yield the prize."

She pulled the Primrose, dipp'd in dawn :
   Its tender odour sweet
Woke gentle lays of childhood's days,
   Ere Time did seem too fleet.

Then to a wood of Hyacinth,
   With willing feet we flew ;
The scented air seemed wrapped in prayer,
   Above the bed of blue.

We sat on banks of violets,
   Dight in the hues of Morn ;
Their balmy breath my being filled,
   Like Love on whispers borne.

Through glades of Hawthorn snow we swept,
   By singing, silvery streams :
The Sun did play on every spray
   With fragrance in his beams.

Here lovers vowed, 'mong tasselled Broom ;
   And, gleaming up the Fell,
The prickly Whin about the linn
   Wafted its creamy smell.

Through fields of Clover, dairy-breath'd,—
   'Neath incense-breathing Pines—
'Mong ruins old, where Tansy bold
   In golden buttons shines.

Then, from a ruined castle bold,
   The fresh Wallflower she flung ;
Till in me rose a clear repose
   And pure deep thoughts unsung.

O'er smooth green hills, where zephyrs bore
  The bleating of the sheep,
We trod on purple fragrant Thyme :
  Elfstoons I fell asleep,
And dreamed a dream within a dream :
  For, bearing Roses white,
A wingéd boy* eastward flew
  To greet Aurora bright.

The blushing goddess of the dawn
  Into her bosom drew
The new-blown Roses,—kiss'd them—then
  To Earth their petals flew ;
But beauteous now as her fair cheek.
  Love gather'd up the flowers,
And strewed the scented damask, round
  His ever blooming bowers.

The Rose filled all my vale of dreams,
  I yielded her the prize :
And Flora like a vision fled
  Before my waking eyes.

---

* Cupid.

TO THE WOOD-SORREL.

(*Oxalis Acetosella.*)

This beauty of the dell is allowed by many authorities to be the real Shamrock of Ireland. About Portrush the writer has often seen it trained in pots in boarding-houses, and was always told it was the Shamrock.

WHEN azure hyacinths perfume
　The woods and greening braes,
With joy I mark thy silken bell—
　Dipped in the morning's rays.
Streaked with Aurora's pencil soft
　Thou art to poet's eye
In thy sweet form, so delicate,
　An image of the sky.
So pensively thy tender form
　In modest beauty blows !
Yea, in the shade, thou tell'st me more
　Than Daffodil or Rose.

TO THE WOODY NIGHTSHADE, OR BITTER-SWEET.*

(*Solanum Dulcemara.*†)

I MAY not sing thy limbs so slender,
Nor thy pale drooping blossoms tender,
But I will chant thy Autumn splendour—
    Solanum Dulcemara !

I know thy home within the glen—
That solemn spot for musing men—
Where o'er thee hops the little wren,
    Solanum Dulcemara !

In Summer when thy lilac bells
Low droop in ferny flowery dells,
And Broom and Hawthorn fling their spells
    About thee—Dulcemara—

Thou seem'st a crouching thing of fear ;
But when the shedding woods grow sere,
Thy glittering clusters then appear—
    Solanum Dulcemara !

For not in glen nor glade, I ween,
Could I such witching berries glean—
Carnation, red, orange, fawn, and green,—
    Solanum Dulcemara !

---

* Nothing can surpass the beauty of its berries in October.
† Meaning—Bitter-sweet.

Frail trailing thing ! Thou hold'st a prize
Each closing year, to glad my eyes ;
And what if there within thee lies
    The germ of Dulcemara ?

May I, like thee, my birthright meet,
And change my bitter into sweet,
And own that Life so frail and fleet
    Is still a " Dulcemara ! "

SONG—MY LOVE.

My love she is a priceless gem
    Which I have envied long :—
A lily on a guarded stem—
    The music of my song :
But I may ne'er that jewel wear
    Upon my ravished breast ;
Nor call that lily fair mine own—
    By noble hands caress'd !

My love is like a berry red
    Beyond the schoolboy's hand ;
A cluster on a palace wall
    Where high birth holds command ;
Would Love me teach, how I might reach
    And pluck that cluster sweet,
I'd happier be than minstrelsy
    With monarchs at its feet !

My love's a flower upon a rock,
    By many a floweret press'd :—
O, I could bear the tempest's shock
    To cull it for my breast :—
Beauty is rare ; and will not share
    Its wealth with low estate :—
So I'll but gaze on Ida's charms
    And mourn my hapless fate !

TO THE QUEEN OF THE MEADOW.

(Spiræa Ulmaria.)

I SAW thee, sweet one, in a dream ;
 And, rising with the morn,
I sought thy home beside the stream—
 Beyond the bladed corn
And the hosts of bearded wheat ;
Where catchy, beauteous, brave, yet fleet,
 Ten thousand poppies met my view,
Fighting their way 'mong coats of green
(No thought of mowing sickles keen)—
 A mimicry of Waterloo—*
 But from the strife I turned to you !

And soon thy stately limbs I spied—
 Laved in a moonbeam bath ; †
Along the meadows I descried
 My queen adorn the brooklet's path—
Where the nettle tried to hide
Thy glory and thy pride ;
 And many a flower would snare
With colours bright my eyes—
Yet hues were not my prize--
 It was thy fragrance rare,
 Thy breath that captive held me there !

---

* Unless the reader has seen a field of green corn glowing with scarlet poppies, he will hardly understand the simile.

† The moonlight colour of the flower.

Queen of the meadow ! Childhood's queen !
  Queen of the air that blows
Adown the lanes and glens so green—
  Floating, like Love, round all that grows—
Filling with unsung witcherie
The heart's deep well that loveth thee !
  O, I would not give the sunny days
With thee and the running brooks
For the treasures of all books,
  Nor aught that flattery says,
  My queen of the wateryways.

TO THE MIGNONETTE.

(*Reseda Odorata.*)

(Language—thy qualities surpass thy charms.)

I HAVE not known thee yet—
Adoréd Mignonette ;
Nor ne'er may understand thy hidden charms
That captivate the air
With soothing odour rare—
Coming like Love that Envy still disarms—
Sweet as a crystal well or maiden's kiss ;
And where thou art, that is a spot of bliss !

How humbly thou dost blow !—
There is no gaudy show
Of colours to allure the wandering eye ;
But gently thou dost smite
Our sense with dear delight,
Which, felt but aye unseen, thou waftest by—
Filling our being with a rich surprise
Like breathings from the vales of Paradise.

Tho' but a lowly flower
Thou speak'st to me with power
Of him who, robed in Mercy, came to save.
He left His starry throne
And wandered wan and lone,
And to the scorn of men Himself He gave ;
Yet Love and Pity were his breath Divine,
Like that pure fragrance and that charm of thine.

TO THE SCOTCH PINE.

(*Pinus Boreallis.*)

BONNETTED warrior of the winds—
　Dark guardian of the glen :
Thy waving plumes amid the blast
　Inspire my raptured pen !　　.

Thy sombre tresses ne'er grow grey
　Nor sere with brown October ;
But round thy ruddy stalwart limbs
　Wave all the year, full sober.

In Spring when all the groves and woods
　In gayest robes are seen,
Their virgin garments brighter shine
　Beside thy dusky green.

Stern, rugged majesty is thine,
　When, anchored to the rock,
Thou laughest while the forest falls
　Beneath the tempest's shock.

But when the fields their fragrance raise
　Round Summer's languid feet—
How healing 'neath thy shade to lie
　And quaff thy incense sweet !

Let Myrtles and fresh Olives spring
　Around the reeling Vine—
Far dearer to the Scottish heart
　Art thou—my Northern Pine !

TO THE POTATO.

(Solanum Tuberosum.)

HAIL—thou that ne'er wast preed by Plato—
My muse wad woo thee, plump Potato,
(Braw cousin to red-robed Tomato
      Sae roun' an' ripe),
Thy worth might draw an obligato
      Frae Pan's sweet pipe !

Dear to the roamin' poet's bosom
Is thy snaw-white or lilac blossom ;
An'—to his een—O rare symposum !—
      Thy stamen's gold !
Thy leaves—solanum tuberosum—
      How rich an' bold !

Thy tubers gust the gab o' a'—
Thou'rt welcome in the cot an' ha',
An' even on royal tables braw
      Thy jacket's seen :—
But, chief, the poor man lo'es thy ba',
      An' laughin' een !

Since great Sir Walter bracht thee new
Frae rainless, gloaminless Peru—
Ma' frien', thou'st been in monie a stew
      At roarin' feasts ;
An' hills o' *thanks* hae risen to you
      Frae gratefu' breasts !

Thou'rt no sae sturdy as the oat—
The bane an' muscle o' the Scot—
Yet, weel supplant'st the parritch pot
    I' the reeky toun,
Whar life drees oot its weary lot
    The hale year roun'.

Lang may yer shaws the drills adorn—
Blythe may yer blossoms greet the morn—
Large be yer bings 'mang stacks o' corn
    At ilk farm door :—
Blank be the day yer held in scorn
    By rich or poor !

TO THE MOUNTAIN VIOLET.
(*Viola Lutea.*)

WHEN Iris, from the mystic light,
    First formed her soft prismatic bow,
Some remnants, by her fingers dight,
    Showered on the wondering Earth below :
The violet's form they did assume—
The whispering air they did perfume !

The sweetest maid e'er poet sung
    Ne'er rivalled thy soft witching charms ;
And, flow'ret, thou art ever young,
    Though Beauty dies in Age's arms :
For Spring still brings thee in his bosom,
And scents the uplands with thy blossom,

Like Amethyst I see thee shine
    On June's rich robe of Roses sweet ;
And Summer's gayrish golds combine
    Thy purple willing nods to greet :
You dance by mountain paths and rills,
And amorous kiss the breathing hills !

Ever, like pleasing Fancy near
    On zepher'd-kiss'd Gleniffer's brow,
I greet thee, each returning year—
    Unchanged as when I made love's vow ;
And thy gay petals softly press'd
Loved Lilyanna's snowy breast !

Ah, sweet Viola ! could my song
    Steal half thy beauty or thy breath,—
Its purer echoes might prolong
    Each cadence past the gate of Death :
Yet aye the Muses, as they roam,
Shall sing around thy mountain home !

LINES

ON SEEING A FIELD OF CURLY GREENS IN BLOSSOM AT PRESTWICK, MAY, 1894.

It is customary for curling clubs in Scotland to challenge each other to a game, the defeated standing "Beef and Greens" in the Village Inn. After some hours at a keen contest on the loch, the appetites of the combatants can do justice to this wholesome repast.

HECH ! what a sicht for poet's e'en !
It's you, my green-powed curly frien' !
Yer surely haudin' holiday ;
Or wad ye welcome winsome May,
That ye hae beat sic yellow fire,
That warms my heart like sweetest choir ?
Your tossing, lowin' dance I see,
Whilk hauds my soul like harmony ;
An' as wi' joy on you I glower,
I feel your beauty's silent power,
And own that frae your gay flirtation
There comes a sweet illumination.

I aye hae counted mang my frien's
A weel how'd plot o' curly greens :
Their palmy blades, the simmer lang,
Are worthy o' some poet's sang.
E'en in Melrose's cloistered shades
I've seen in stane their feather'd blades
Adorn a pillar, staunin' still
A monument o' sculptor's skill.

But let me sing o' guid digestion,
And ask this gastronomic question :
In winter, whan the North bites sair
An' wigs the woods wi' cranreugh hair,

Whan skiters skite an' curlers roar,
An' gloamin' greets some merry corp
Planted fu' snug in Luckie's " Best,"
Wi' appetites that winna rest—
Wad Esculapius fret or froon
Whan " beef an' greens " the table croon ;
An' reekin' taties burst their graith,
An' ilka man hauf hauds his breath
Till cosilie the table's laid
An' presidential grace is said ?

Let jaupy soups sour'd stomachs rake !
But beef an' greens an' crumpy cake
Are Scotland's wintery doctor's kist ;
Wi' langkail * may she lang be blessed.

---

* Langkail is the *German* or *curly* green, boiled and mashed ;
usually eaten with oaten cakes.

TO THE HAWTHORN, OR MAY BLOSSOM.

(*Cratægus Oxyacantha.*)

ABOVE the Broom's bright golden glow
Again thou shower'st thy fragrant snow,
And round the brows of Spring dost throw
    Thy garland white ;
And through my spirit thou dost blow
    Hope's dear delight.

O, joy ! as through the glen I stray,
To mark thy purple Anthers gay
Amid thy creamy petals play
    So beauteous fair,
And feel how sweet thy breath, O May,
    Holds all the air.

I fly the City's ways uncouth,
And, 'neath thy angel wings of Ruth,
I clasp the memories of Youth—
    Dear Hawthorn flower—
And feel the simple love and truth
    Of Childhood's hour !

Though crazy Age steals on full fleet,
The years shall find thee young and sweet ;
And children's little prattling feet
    Shall round thee play,
And their clear merry laughter greet
    Thy blossoms gay !

TO THE RED CAMPION.

(Lychnis Diurna.)

LIKE a little rosy maiden,
　Peeping through the ferny brake,
In thy robes so downy laden—
　All the woods sing for thy sake :
　　Thou art sure a ruby set
　　In the spring's gay coronet.

'Mong the hyacinth's bright blue,
　And the stitchwort's stars so white,
There in spring I look for you,
　Shewing off your petals bright—
　　With the muses set me free,
　　Wooing such a galaxy.

Thou dost blush the cheek of May,
　As she walks in white and gold ;
While the brackens on the brae
　Ope their fronds so manifold—
　　Bowing, through the sunny hours,
　　Adoration to the flowers.

Campion, thou dost court the sun ;
　And the insects of a day
O'er thy ruddy blossoms run,
　Seeking still their honied way—
　　You and they, with little strife,
　　Linking still the chain of life.

TO THE WHITE CAMPION.

(*Lychnis Vespertina.*)

This handsome flower opens only in the night, when it then gives forth a sweet perfume. Its snowy petals and delicious fragrance attract night moths, which fertilise it. At dawn of day the flowers fold up, and by noon seem dead and withered; but at evening they again unfold their charms; and so on for several nights, until they require no more help of the moths, and then they die.

DEAR Lychnis Vespertina ! soothing name !
   Who woos thy breath, salutes the evening star !
By day thy sister with the sun dost flame,
   But thou ne'er court'st the triumphs of his car.

Beneath pale Luna's silent, silvery sway
   Thou swingest incense to the nightingale,
And 'neath the influence of the Milkyway
   Thou pourest odours from thy blossoms pale.

Dotting the silent wilderness of night,
   Thy snowy blooms still mark where moths do play ;
But when the garish day with flowers is bright,
   Thou veil'st thy form in semblance of decay.

So that the anxious bee and butterfly
   Do pass thee by as beauty long since dead ;
But fairy Science can thy ways descry
   As she sits peering by thy noonday bed.

Thy rosy sister hoards diurnal wealth ;
   Thou, like a student, burn'st the midnight oil—
Yea, all things living, by some wondrous stealth,
   For happy life do ever onwards toil.

VOICES OF NATURE.

I.

How varied the voices of Nature—
  What a winning speech hath she—
From the treble of rills 'mong the heathery hills
  To the roar of the restless sea !

When the virgin Spring comes smiling,
  And her fingers the fresh flowers strew,—
From the Primrose dells how each warbler tells
  His love to his love anew !

Let us up through the glen, soft shaded,
  Where the Hyacinth's smoke exhales
Its perfume sweet all about our feet,
  And the Throstle betunes the gales.

O, list, till the soul grows full,
  By the cascade's rush and din—
To the hiss of its spray—like an alto's lay—
  And the bass of its boulder'd linn !

Far away 'mong the scented fields
  We will learn of the bee's sweet psalm,
As she ringeth the hours on the bells of flowers
  When the summer days are calm !

O, hark, how the Lark is storming
  The gates of Heaven with song :—
On his choral wing how he longs to sing
  In the midst of its blissful throng.

But the Autumn hath donned her robe ;
   All the birds are mute—save he
Of the ruddy breast : but he now sings best,
   For he trilleth so mournfully.

II.

Go, pace, entranced, the forest's faded fanes,
   When Winter winds usurp mild Autumn's choir ;
And from the boles what deep and solemn strains
   Awaken in our breast true worship's fire !

III.

Ten thousand torrents, that did lakeward leap,
   Or sang, in solo, to the silent Pine,—
United are, that voice that knows not sleep—
   Niagara booming to the boundless Brine !

.   .   .   .

With awe o'erwhelmed, bow down my wondering soul—
   The Almighty's Thunder, hurtling hurls on high !—
'Tis God that speaks amid that solemn roll—
   His Majesty of Glory passeth by !

MAUD MUNROE.

(A MEMORY.)

A VISION comes of long ago !
  I see it flit about the Mill—
The lovely form of Maud Munroe,
  As witching as the Daffodil !

Her cheeks were Daisies at the dawn,
  Her bosom the Camelia's snow ;
And blythely tripp'd the dewy lawn
  The fairy feet of Maud Munroe.

Ripe berries of the Guelder Rose
  Recall her lips ; and her bright eyes—
Twin Brambles black, when Autumn throws
  Across the vales her myriad dyes :—

While, dangling with delight, aye blew
  About her graceful, ivory shoulder,
Rich curls of deepest hazel hue,
  Like clustered Blue-bells o'er a boulder.

The very waving of her gown
  Was like a Lady Birch in June,
That rains its fragrant foliage down
  As Zephyrs through it sing a tune.

Not sweeter sang the Thrush in Spring,
  Above the creamy mantled Sloe ;
No Lark, on heaven-aspiring wing,
  Ere thrilled my soul like Maud Munroe !

Till I had met this nymph of light,
    My heart slept like a Summer linn ;
But swift Love's torrent, in its might,
    Stirred all its depths, such prize to win !

.   .   .   .   .   .

But such a gleam of heavenly rays
    Too lovely grew for mortal's eye !
The sun still on the brooklet plays—
    And Maud Munroe sings from the sky !

Yet aye as by the Mill I stray,
    And scent the Roses, newly blown—
Or, musing, climb the flowery brae—
    I see her still on Beauty's throne !

MAY.

Room for the Queen! She comes, with robes inwrought
With purple and fine gold. In her white hand
How bright her Caltha burns! Her Hawthorn breath
Makes glad the hearts of swains and maidens fair!
Hail to the Queen! She comes with flowery train.
Among her Daisy suns she trips, and o'er
The fragrant carpets of the field she walks,
While zephyrs kiss her dimpled virgin cheek
And wave her Lilac gown—with violets trimmed,
Gay flounced with yellow Broom. Her peerless eyes
Of bright Veronica beheld with joy
The glades herself adorns!

       To greet their Queen
The furzy fields flame far their fragrant blooms ;
While to the jocund sun the Chestnut towers
Her silvery candelabra, and the lawns
In Rhododendron splendour gorgeous glow!

All hail, sweet May! Hail, Vestal of the year!
Come, spread thy azure mantle 'neath our woods,
Made vocal by thy smile. Thou bringest still
Young rural Joy, with sweetest odours fanned.
The citron Primrose and the Woodruff fling
Their beauty and their perfume round thy feet
Soft sandalled with all flowers of lovely hue.
Thy brows are wreathed in pure immortal Youth!

TO THE YELLOW BEDSTRAW, OR LADIES BEDSTRAW.

(ORIGINALLY "OUR LADY'S BEDSTRAW.")

(Galium Verum.)

Many of the wild flowers are dedicated to the Virgin—and in all such cases the prefix should be "Our Lady's" instead of "Ladies'."

WHEN the hay is a-coiling, perfuming the breeze,—
    Far over the uplands I wander,
Where the pure azure Hairbells are swung by the bees,
    And, like Fancy, the streamlets meander :

For I know I shall gather thy glorified gold—
    To panicled splendour sunbeaten ;
And feel that thy breath, as in summers of old,
    The wings of the zephyr doth sweeten.

How loving I linger, allured by thy charms—
    My lips with the Blaeberry dying :—
And I now seem to clasp Mother Earth in my arms,
    While around me the streamlets are sighing.

For the "Bless'd among women" our sires did thee
    name ;
    And a sanctity circles thy beauty :
And may I, in the light of thy pure golden flame,
    Still walk in the pathway of Duty.

SONG—UNDER THE MISTLETOE.

UNDER the Mistletoe's pearly boughs,
   There we in silence plighted;
Your quick glance flashed 'neath your snowy brows
   That was never by sorrow blighted.

Under the Holly, with Coral crowned,
   Two loving hearts grew single :
We, by the pearls of the mistletoe bound,
   In the ocean of Love did mingle !

IN OCTOBER.

CORN-YELLOW all things look ; the Light
That waved, in Summer, angel white,
Is with the mellow hue bedight.

Skirting the stream, that softly choirs,
The Beech has lit her farewell fires
Beneath the Poplar's amber spires—

Whose leaves, when fitful breezes wake,
All pattering, dancing, shimmering shake,
Like big rain o'er a sleeping lake.

The Ash, the last to don her green,
To greet the Springtime's flowery scene,
Doffs first her fading robes, I ween !

Where warm the dark-brown Brackens lie,
The Bramble peers like maiden shy
Bewitching with her raven eye !

The Rose hangs out her ruby lamps,
Tho' death o'er Flora's beauty tramps,
And with " Decay " the Lovely stamps !

The glens are hushed !   No vocal vows
Are heard from birds among the boughs—
Sad Pensiveness wreaths Nature's brows !—

For Winter, with his icy spear,
In snowy mantle draweth near
To triumph o'er the sickly year !

AN ALPHABET OF TREES.

For the Children.

A—is the Ash—holds our hammer-head fast.
B—is the Beech—gave our forefathers Mast.*
C—is the Chestnut—with shoe of the horse.
D—shows the Dryads—sweet Woods Nymphs, of course.
E—is the Elm—tall and handsome, I ween.
F—is the Fir—ever fragrant and green.
G—is the Gean-tree, which schoolboys know.
H—is the Hornbeam—leaves silvered below.
I—is the Ilex—a name for the Holly.
J—is the Juniper—dark, melancholy!
K—is the Kissing-tree—bless'd among trees.
L—is the Lime—a great Minster for bees.
M—is the Maple—gives sugar refined.
N—Noble-bay—Roman brows used to bind.
O—is an Oak, when a thousand years speed.
P—is the Plane that hath wings on its seed.
Q—is the Quince—fruit in jam often found.
R—is the Rowan—for beauty renowned.
S—Service-tree—and it takes a rich polish.
T—Tree of Liberty—who dare demolish?
U—is the Upas—right deadly, I ween!
V—is the Vine-tree, at Hampton Court seen.
W—Willows by waters aye wailing.
X—Xylobalsamum—perfume exhaling.
Y—is the Yew—ever gloomy and sad.
Z—Zebra-wood—maketh joiners' hearts glad.
& so, my dear children, here endeth my fad!

---

* The Beech Nuts.

TO A BEECH TREE IN OCTOBER.

HAIL ! *nec tamen consumebatur !*—
  Lov'd flame of the forest once green !
How November thy glory shall scatter—
  And I'll sigh for the light that hath been.

In thy yellow-green robe in the Spring time—
  To me thy soft mantle was dear ;
But I love thee to-day in thy garb of Decay
  And thy crown of rich beauty all sere !

THE POET'S RAMBLE IN OCTOBER.

RIPE are October's glories : Come away !
Hushed are the waiting woods : their rustling robes
Of mildest tints, create within my soul
Emotions meet for melancholy song !
See, Winter in white robes, with icy spear,
Comes slowly o'er the northern hills—snow-capp'd.
Then pause with Nature, ye that live estranged
Amid the city's roar ; and list the voice
That calls you forth to cull emotions sweet,
And gaze entranced across the garnished woods.
Mark how the forest now hath doffed its green,
And Nature dons her cloak of many hues ;
Now reigns the holy beauty of Decay !
How calmly sleeps the lake : the coloured woods
Reflected on its face in thousand tints
Now flash across that dome of thought—the mind—
And brighter lift Imagination's eye.
Like rainbows wreck'd, all the gay woods do sing,
The Hawthorn hedge gleams like the Pheasant's breast.

Its silvery candelabra's lights long out
The Chestnut sweeps, in saffron hues, the lawn.
Skirting the field the Whin, repellant, throws
His golden offering at grim Winter's feet ;
And, " beautiful for ever," daisies lift
Their sleepy eyes to the receding sun.

See how Betula dreams herself away,
Or showers her myriad leaves on brakens brown ;
Sambucas, glittering, floods the groves with wine.

Mark how yon boulder with the bramble burns,
It's jetty blobs, like eyes, peer from the grass ;
And here and there along its spiny arms,
A spray of silken blossoms yet appears—
Like aged Laurette, crowned with fruit of song,
Still waking music in his country's heart.

Lo, the pale Poplar—like an amber tower—
Quivers beneath the Beech's flaming flag ;
The Oak, by summer's scorching rays, hath tanned
His rugged face beside the late-robed Ash,
Whose garments heavy drop in faded green
Among the Rose's scarlet lamps—the hips—
That to the now mute birds are light and food.

Winding the boles th' immortal Ivy clings ;
And, sombre, over all the sturdy Pine,
Expectant, waits its robe of ermine snow.

From out yon nimbus cloud, the mighty sun
Sweeps o'er the raptured woods his golden beams,
And wakens in my soul such dulcet chords
As harp or breathing organ never swelled.

O, what a charm hath Nature for her child !
Let me but lie upon her matron lap
And gaze adoring on her lovely face—
The reflex of my God—and I am bless'd !

OCTOBER.

Come, dowie October, in mantle o' yellow,
  Wi' the Hyp an' the Haw on thy fast-fading croon ;
Come, soothe me a blink wi' thy speech sad and mellow,
  As 'mang the brown Brackens I saft lay me doun !

O, lay on my lips—frae the Simmer sun droothie—
  Ae blab o' the Bramble, November shall mar ;
An' read me yer sermon sae saftly an' coothie,
  While draps the last Row'n in the deep rocky scaur !

Thou tell'st me the friens that I loo'd in Life's Simmer,
  Like thy chequered leaves frae my heart drap awa' ;
An' leave, o' the licht o' ilk face, but a glimmer,
  Aboon the wild waste o' Death's drear driftin' snaw !

October, I lo'e thee ! Thy whisper is soothing ;
  There is Lore in thy face, there is wealth in thy
      bowers :
Thy pensiveness adds but a charm to my musing—
  And sweet are my dreams through thy fast ebbing
      hours !

LINES

On meeting in a railway train a little Highland maid from Tighnabruaich : she was carrying with peculiar care a large bouquet of garden
flowers to a sick friend in Glasgow.

SWEET flower of Tighnabruaich's shade !
Queen Flora sends thee, little maid,
To bear those living treasures bright
To give thy dear sick friend delight :
But sure naught sweeter may she see
Than thy sweet face : for even to me
A charm about thy English rung—
Soft cadenced by thy Gaelic tongue !

Lo ! what thy posie doth display !—
Great Marigolds, with wealth all gay,
Pyrethyrums with frizzy locks,
And white and lilac scented Phlox :
Spiræas, brought from queer Japan,
Rear high their sculptured steeples wan,
And Poppies red from orient fields
Whose milky juice " Oblivion " yields.

But, on thy Bouquet's summit, blows
The image of thyself—the Rose :
'Tis not more fair when, on its thorn,
It spreads its bosom to the morn—
Wiping the tears of night away—
And, blushing, greets the lord of Day
Than thou in thy parental shade,
My lovely little Highland maid.

Glad Innocence and Beauty blend
About thy brow.   Go, lightly tend
Thy lambs that crop the fresh green grass,
Till thou to womanhood shall pass ;
Then may thy cheeks—by young Love's flame,
Bear blossoms that the Heathbells shame ;
Till some strong shepherd claims thy heart,
And only death your loves shall part !

CHRISTMAS.

HEAR we to-day how the angels are singing
  All through the wynds and the dusky lanes?
Over the earth they are chorally winging—
  White are their wings 'mid the world's foul stains.
The angels are with us—they are hovering near—
  Hark how they carol their Christmas cheer!
And, look! Night's brow wears a glorious gem,
For it beareth the Star of Bethlehem.

Charity, Mercy, Truth, we now welcome you;
  Down from the Throne with the Christ ye once came;
Long through the night we have heard the clear song
      of you,
  O, let such music our freezing hearts flame!
Hate, o'er the rim of the earth be hurled—
Christ's banner of Love it is now unfurled!
O, see! Night's brow bears a glorious gem—
Earth knows it—the Planet of Bethlehem.

Bring pearls of the Mistletoe, coral of Holly,
  And hang them aloft in the cot and the hall;
Let Joy now banish dark-eyed Melancholy,
  And every heart ope' where the angels' feet fall.
Old Night turns Day in the light of that gem—
The wondrous Star of Bethlehem.

In Memoriam:

ROBERT FULTON CRAIG, *died at Caversbank House, Paisley, on 5th May, 1894, in the fortieth year of his age.*

My late lamented friend was an ardent admirer and student of Nature, and in field botany he had few equals in and around Paisley. I can never forget the many delightful chats I had with him on the names and haunts of the wild flowers. His love of the wildlings sweetened his whole life.

DEAR brother—that did'st love the lowliest flower
    That weeps its dewdrops o'er thy slumbering clay,
I think of thee, full clad in manhood's dower,
    Laid low by envious Death in Life's noonday;
And, with the fragrance of the bird-tuned May,
    I, too, above thy bier some song-drops shed:
Thou, that through flowerland oft did with us stray,
    We cannot deem thy face for aye hath fled
Into the doleful chambers of the dead.

O, lovely flowers—more beauteous by the love
    He bore to you—wave o'er his mansion cold,
Yet know his spirit hovers still above
    Your varied sweets and forms so manifold;
Spread all your wealth of purple and of gold
    In tribute to the praise he poured on you.
The tongue that ever of your charms was bold
    Is silent now; nor can his eyes once view
    Your myriad tints the lovely landscape strew.

Ye daisies, that do claim the changeful year,
  Watch by the bed of him who loved you well ;
Ye snowdrops, that bring Hope with eyes so clear,
  Come bless our winter, and our sad hearts tell
That he who in Life's fray too early fell
  Lives far aloft, where never-fading flowers
Bloom by the stream where all the faithful dwell,
  Where Time is not, nor sorrow's sable hours,
  But bliss abides in white radanthine bowers.

TO THE MEMORY OF BURNS.

This garland is made up according to the "Language of Flowers."

Read at the Paisley Burns Club Supper, County Hotel, Paisley, January 25, 1893.

THE trembling Muse, with fond desire,
    Again would weave a garland fair
Of flowerets, round the golden lyre
    Whose music sweetens Scotia's air !
We'll crown the Bard with wildling flowers
    From field and fen, from dale and dell,
From sylvan shades and woodbine bowers,
    From heathy moor and lofty fell.
The Ivy in his garland twine—
    The type of his immortal lays—
And wreathe it 'mong the Eglantine,
    Dark-eyed Magnolias and Bays.
Its pearls shall be fresh Daisy gems
    And Cowslips wet with morning dew,
And Speedwells on their slender stems,
    And Hyacinths and Harebells blue.
An ear of Wheat for wealth of song,
    The Snowdrop for his soaring hopes,
And Oak leaves for his manhood strong,
    And sprig of Pine, that Pity props.
Fresh Pansies for his thoughts sublime,
    And purple Heath for Solitude ;
And for his Courage fragrant Thyme,
    And Lilies for his love of Good.
A leaf from off the spreading Plane
    Shall symbolise his Genius bright ;

And so we crown with flowers again
  The memory of his natal night !
Tho' down the drumly tide of Time
  Forgetfulness still bears along
Full many a faintly-fading chime
  Of what an age deemed " deathless song ! "
Yet, radiant thro' the dark'ning Past,
  And glorious thro' the dust of urns,
There shines a star no clouds o'ercast—
  The deathless fame of Robert Burns !

OCTOBER MUSINGS.

I SAW the poet, pensive, musing, stray
    Amid the glories of October's portals.
Bright crimson fruits shone far in bright array—
    While falling leaves bespoke the life of mortals !
The Beech flashed far its flame o'er fading woods—
    Fading, yet fragrant, and of many a hue—
(Fit emblem of the poet's varied moods)
    While dappled clouds sailed o'er their sea of blue.
I marked the singer ; and his look was sad,
    And on his shoulder leaned the pensive muse
In garland of red berries, and full clad
    In russet garments of a thousand hues.
With pensive smile she bade him touch his lyre
    In saddened tones amid the rustling bowers :
Her speech awoke in him new choral fire—
    And thus he mourned farewell to Summer's flowers :

" Adieu, my summer flowers ! a fond adieu !
    I loved ye as ye danced by field and stream ;
I love ye now—receding far from view—
    I love ye when awake or when I dream !
O, bright and beauteous train ! ye would not stay ;
    Yet, vanished all, hear now my sad farewell.
I see ye, linked together, far away,
    Yet in my heart I feel your holy spell !
' O, Hyacinthus, in thy robe of sky—
    O, saffron Primula—Spring's darling pride—
O, gold-crowned Celandine—how quick ye hie !
    Ye sweet breathed queens, far from my gaze ye glide

O, tasselled Broom, the music of the Bard—
  O, stately Foxgloves guarding daisied fields ;
And Hawthorn, Thyme, perfuming glen and sward—
  Your mem'ries now a sudden solace yields !

Come mild October, mellow, meek, demure ;
  Drop in my vacant heart thy soothing treasures ;
Thy woodland gardens make the spirit pure
  And strike to sober tones the poet's measures !

Yet, hope shall burn 'neath Winter's icy load,
  That Flora's children I again may meet
To cheer me on Life's weary winding road,
  And bathe my being in their charms so sweet !

ODE TO OCTOBER.

OCTOBER, russet matron of the year,—
    Waving adieu to Autumn's golden train—
Spreading abroad thy banner red and sere
    To welcome Winter from the north again—
    I offer you the tribute of a strain ;
(Of all the pacing months thou'rt dearly mine)
    To sing thy praise the muse may ne'er refrain,
Or round thy sober brows red berries twine,
Half hid in Holly smooth, and scented sprigs of Pine.

Now, in thy cloak of countless shades and mild,
    Thou marchest to the music of soft winds ;
The ruddy Beech, of all its green beguiled,
    Beneath the tawny Oak a shelter finds ;
    And the broad Elm—full many a wreath it binds
To float upon the brooklet's bosom fair—
    Pensive as thoughts that glide thro' pensive minds—
Mellow as mellowed words such thoughts prepare—
Soft as the voice of Love, borne on thy evening air.

Thy woods, full radiant as the Iris, glow
    With witching tints—unknown to Summer's flowers ;
Red, brown, and yellow, with green lawns below,
    And crimsoned clusters in the Nightshade bowers ;
    While o'er the dreamy vale the dark Pine towers,
And hedgerows gleam in purple fringed with gold—
    Singing harmonious to the breezy hours—
Making the year seem young, tho' growing old ;
So Love grows sober as our years are told !

Thou hast a grace the poet's bosom warms ;
   'Tis said that he who sung our Bliss once lost,
Whene'er he felt thy ever soothing charms
   Uttered divinest song—now England's boast !
   Even Love himself in thee is loving most,
When moonbeams play among the village trees
   And rustling leaves by tiny feet are crossed,
And the young-old tale falls like thy whispering breeze :
So come all seasons, the pure mind to please.

NOVEMBER.

SPRING'S wakening bugle long is hushed,
  Long dimm'd is Summer's splendour ;
October yields her easel bright
  To " black and white " November !

Even so—the hopes of boyhood,
  But few I do remember :
The hills of fame I meant to scale
  Grow misty in November !

The faces and the friends long fled,
  Grow paler, dimmer, slender ;
The tones of love once pleasing heard,
  Grow echoes in November !

But woods and lanes that seemed so green
  In childhood's springtime season ;
Seem fairer now, by Fancy sunned,
  And beautified by Reason !

Those starry hosts—the fields of flowers—
  Fierce Boreas may dismember ;
But thou doth deck thy sombre brows
  With countless stars, November.

If jocund Spring doth singing come
  In clouds of hawthorn blossom ;
Yet old November oft doth wear
  The snowflake on his bosom !

If, in my youth, the world seemed young—
    Experience is a treasure
Which, put to usury, may bring
    To middle life a pleasure !—

And when with age the house shall fall,
    The tenant hath grown richer :—
The fount of life for ever flows,
    Though broken lies the pitcher.

WINTER.

MUST I, the wildling's singer, end
  My song, when o'er their wintry sleep
The fleecy blasts their curtains bend
  In requiem folds ? Must I, too, weep ?
And dreary dirges urge my quill
To mourn decay o'er wood and hill ?

Nay ! Let my song with Hope be bold !
  'Neath Winter's shroud the Daisy waits
To rise, a citadel of gold
  Girt with a hundred pearly gates :
And fragrant herbs shall odours swing
About the lovely feet of Spring !

As sudden as the shepherds' eyes
  Beheld the angels long ago ;
So shall I see with glad surprise
  The hosts of snowdrops beauteous blow
About the woods : sweet things of hope
That come Queen Flora's halls to ope !

Then, o'er the snows of Winter strew
  The memories of Summer's flowers ;
And deem that Love that love once drew
  Lies sleeping warm in Eden bowers ;
The chilling blast we misname Death
Hath future life in its cold breath !

BLOOMS AND SPRAYS FROM HOLY WRIT.

No. 1.—THE ROSE.

"I am the Rose of Sharon," Cant. II., I.

THE traveller, weary by the way,
　　Doth oft forget his wants and woes,
As round him, 'neath noon's burning ray,
　　Soft wafts the fragrance from the Rose.

So to the pilgrim, Zion bound,
　　From Sharon's Rose sweet odours steal,
To make his pathway hallowed ground ;
　　And foretastes of his rest reveal.

How lovely are the lays that rise
　　Around the Rose, on Beauty's throne !
A maiden queen, she holds all eyes,
　　And all her heavenly fragrance own :—

But purer strains eternal ring
　　From saints below and saints above ;
And hosts unnumbered praise their King
　　Who bears the fragrant name of Love !

No. 2.—THE LILY.

"I am . . . a Lily of the Valley."—Cant. II., I.

THE loveliness of Love doth blow
　　Where'er the Lily rears her head ;
Where she unfolds her fragrant snow
　　All sweetest sanctities are shed.

She courts the dell, in lowly guise,
   Nor armoured as the Rose is she ;
She captive holds admiring eyes,
   And Beauty is her panoply !

Whene'er I mark the Lily fair,
   I see One, radiant as the morn,
Bend o'er her ; and, with accents rare,
   Her glory with His own adorn !

Yea, comlier far, more glorified,
   Was He who graced Earth's sinful vale ;
The flower of Love—the Crucified—
   Was lovelier than the Lily pale !

No. 3.—To a Cedar of Lebanon.

"The Righteous shall grow like a Cedar in Lebanon."—Ps. xcii., 12.
The Arabs say that the Cedar never dies. It is known to live for thousands of years.

Majestic emblem of the good,
   Robed in unfading dress !
What strains shall sing thy ancient power
   And regal loftiness ?

For still thy fragrant branches wave
   On Lebanon's bold brow ;
And such as Hebrew bards inspired
   So is thy glory now !

Thy grandeur and thy beauty tower
   Firm rooted to the rock :—
The war of winds and shafts of time
   Thy calm repose doth mock !

The canker worm ne'er blights thy bole—
   Strong symbol of the Just :
Thou bloom'st secure when impious thrones
   Are turned to common dust !

Prophetic tree ! For aye the type
   Of Righteousness and Truth
That grow not old—but like to thee
   Bloom in immortal Youth—

Shedding pure odours all around :
   A shade for the oppressed !
A plenitude of saintliness
   In God's own beauty dressed !

No. 4.—THE DATE PALM.

"The Righteous shall flourish like the Palm tree."—Ps. xcii., 12.

THE Cedar and the Oak o'erawe !
   The Palm doth admiration wake !
From hidden springs its roots still draw
   The sap that makes it fruitful shake.

Type of the upright man, that grows
   Amid Life's weary desert waste :—
His soul no dearth of bounty knows—
   Fed from the secret wells of Grace.

When weary-footed Israel marched
 Through burning sand without a glade !
Their weary hosts, all dry and parched,
 Drank Elim's wells—felt Elim's shade.

So oft when by the world oppressed
 Some sweetly shaded spot is ours :—
A place of wells and quiet rest—
 Beneath Contentment's palmy bowers !

Around thee, Palm, what memories hang,
 Choral, as round thy flowers the bees :—
Thy praise through Zion's temple rang—
 Thou art the Poetry of Trees !

THE FLOWERS WILL COME AGAIN.

(A WINTER SOLACE.)

O, HEART, what gives thee pain ?—
Though Winter, waring, reign—
The woods with bells of blue shall ring
A welcome to young laughing Spring—
　　The flowers will come again !

O, heart, what gives thee pain ?—
Like Beauty without stain
The Primrose shall thy fancy hold
Beside the brooklet clear and cold—
　　The flowers will come again !

O, heart, what gives thee pain ?—
Lured by the Throstle's strain
To hawthorn glades thou wilt repair
And many a flower shall greet thee there—
　　All these will come again !

O, heart, what gives thee pain ?—
With Roses in her train
Queen Summer comes, with lilies crowned
And heath-bells round her temples bound—
　　The flowers will come again !

O, heart, what gives thee pain ?—
Thine is a countless gain !
Dear, tender Nature grows not old,
And lavish is her lap of gold—
　　The flowers will come again !

MISCELLANEOUS POEMS.

(SOME OF LOCAL INTEREST ONLY.)

VICTORIA.

See, Liberty, enthroned on sweetest flowers,
　　Ascends, with burnished trump, the fair June skies,
And wide around the Earth her music showers,
　　Bidding the nations wake with glad surprise,
And shout with her in accents of the free,
In loftiest tones, " Victoria's Jubilee ! "

First glad Britannia loud the anthem swells
　　"God save the Queen,"—and with a glowing pride
She chants her victories and each triumph tells
　　In Arts or War, or where her great ships ride
On every wave—to set the captive free :
And sings, with grateful heart, " Victoria's Jubilee ! "

Then high above the Atlantic's surge and roar
　　In England's tongue Columbia's shout ascends.;
While echoing to Pacific's utmost shore
　　A youngling continent her greeting sends
To bless a Queen who rules none but the free—
" All hail Victoria Queen !　Hail to thy Jubilee ! "

Loud o'er the wreck of Juggernaut's red car
　　Dark India triumphs in her Empress Queen,
And, hopeful, marks the lustre of her star—
　　The brightest that our Earth hath ever seen :

And darker Africa, whose sons are free,
Swells gratefully the hymn—" Victoria's Jubilee !"

Ye tyrants who bear ill your heavy load,
  Our Queen o'er you the robe of pity throws;
Then hither come—tho' long and rough the road,
  And breathe the fragrance of an English Rose
That for six decades hath adorned a throne
Whose splendour grateful Earth this joyous day doth
    own.

TO STAFFA.

VISITED AUGUST 1869.

AND is this Staffa ? This the cavern vast
  Which oft in boyhood's years I longed to see—
And am I 'neath its vaulted roof at last
  List'ning the ocean's murm'ring melody ?
Ah yes! and while I view such grandeur bold
I find to me the half had not been told !

O aged Staffa—with thy wondrous cave—
  Since first dread Pluto reared thy columns fair
And belched thee glowing—thro' the troubled wave
  Smiting the dark'ning sky with sudden glare—
Full oft thou hast repell'd the surging tide
And all unmovéd viewed the tempest's pride !

Long e're those Desert piles arose to view
  That hide the dust of Egypt's mighty kings
Or yet the fame of proud Serapis grew
  (When Time reigned young o'er all created things)
Full many a storm had scathed thy summit hoar
And thy dark aisles rebellowed ocean's roar !

Thy sister, fair Iona—like a queen
  Once robed in saintly beauty—what is she ?—
A place where men now wonder what hath been ;
  While thou—as time defying as the sea—
Unreared by human hands, doth proudly smile
While man's great temples rise and fall the while !

Hail ! hoary Staffa ! Temple of the wave—
  Treading thy altar steps with weary moan
Old Neptune as thy priest, still holds thy nave ;
  His ancient voice here echoes sad and lone—
Or, brimmed with awful mirth that voice he'll raise
Till all thy pillar'd fanes shall thunder glorious praise !

THE BARDS OF PAISLEY.

If corroboration were needed of the saying that Paisley has pro-
duced more poets than any town of its size, it is to be found in the
pages of "The Poets of Paisley," by the late ex-Provost Brown, where
a brief sketch is given of the life and verses of no fewer than two
hundred and twenty-four bards, all either born or naturalised in the
town. When it is considered that nearly all of these lived and sang
during the present century, and published in whole or part, we must
conclude with William Motherwell, that "Paisley is a veritable nest
of singing birds."

INVERNESS for *English* speakers ;
Oban for its pleasure seekers ;
Paisley for its maidens fair—
And bards, their praises to declare.

High favoured town—Apollo's throne—
Gleniffer's still thy Helicon,
As when upon the Weaver * fell
Fair Fancy's mantle, by the well.

---

* Tannahill.

There yearly through the broom I mount,
To taste that pure Castalian fount ;
There murmur by the Linn's deep roar,
Or gaze the enchanting landscape o'er.

Saint Mirrin, why should I once lift
My pen to praise thy warbling gift ?
The echo of thy song is bless'd—
I pledge thee, minstrel of the west !

Long may the Nine, that shining throng,
Still bathe thee in the light of song ;
And on the ear of Fame still beat
The silvery music of their feet.

FACES.

Each man I meet, unconscious oft,
    Is ever reading books—
Not writ with ink, in leather bound,
    But his brother's changeful looks !

What histories and strange romance,
    What Agonies, what Graces,
We ever read from life till death
    Deep penned on human faces !

I pace the city's hustling streets,
    Where Life's keen battle wages,
And read each soldier's countenance
    That in the strife engages !—

Glad Hope, fell Fear, Mistrust and Guilt,
　　Mad Laughter, Smiles, and Tears,
And cold Disdain, and hateful Pride,
　　And faces ploughed with years !

There, see the anxious merchant speed—
　　With Cunning in his eyes ;
Here struts the Student, book in hand—
　　His look doth clutch the prize !

Here Disappointment's doleful look,
　　Wandering it knows not where :
And she, long lost to chastity—
　　With face set like a snare !

And yonder lurks the stealthy thief—
　　His visage changing ever—
Still simulating every face :—
　　The Taker—ne'er the Giver !

With slanting brow and open mouth,
　　Swings brainless Jollity ;
And on its arm bland Opulence—
　　A face most sad to see !

See ! wan and weary, sunken-eyed,
　　There crawleth wrinkled Care ;
And on his track with blood-shot eyes
　　There staggers wild Despair.

Here, wicks of mouth still earwards bent,
　　His coat long out of date,
Slow creeps the Miser, and behind,
　　With teeth on edge, grins Hate.

Mark this cold form, of No-heart born,
　With face unlined and smug—
The Heartless man, with Callousness
　Around him like a rug.

There goes the Stoic, unconcern
　Stamped on his forehead aye ;
And Hunger with his sunken cheek
　From door to door doth stray.

Look ! all his avenues agape—
　Eyes starting from their sockets—
That's Wonder ; and anear is Theft
　A-picking of his pockets.

There walks the Maiden, " Fancy free,"
　Her cheeks a dawn in May ;
One passing glimpse of that sweet face
　Might make a sad heart gay.

Here, arm in arm, two seem but one—
　And *that* the cooing dove—
Their faces like a dream illumed
　By the languorous light of Love.

And there walks he, the Gifted one,
　He moves with conscious grace—
The Poet ; but can words define
　The language of *his* face ?

Ah ! you and I, unconscious oft,
　Are reading aye such books :
But what sweet charmèd pen can tell
　What flits in human Looks !

ODE TO TRUTH.

TWIN spirit of the Light,
Fair baffler of old Night,
That round thee still would throw his sable pall,
But ne'er shall once caress
Thy holy loveliness,
Nor touch those limbs that angel eyes enthral :
No dawn ere rose upon thy forehead fair,
Nor can seraphic hymns' thy comeliness declare.

More glorious than the sun—
What conquests hast thou won !—
Foul sin and shame thy eyes can ne'er abide.
In direful overthrow,
Old Error, Guilt, and Woe,
Beneath Oblivion, at thy glance do hide ;
At thy command the red-robed tyrant reels
To black perdition's depths, beneath thy chariot wheels.

Sweet to the poet's ear
Come thy pure accents clear,
As, seeking thee, he roams o'er hill and vale ;
Perchance to catch one glance
Of thy fair countenance
In leaf and flower, or scent thee in the gale ;
Or catch thee floating on some rainbowed wing,
Or see thy peerless form in some clear gurgling spring.

With joy thou dost surprise
Her of the myriad eyes—
Fair Science, seeking still thy 'witching face
Through clouds of mystery,
In air and earth and sea,
Or down the far-lit lanes of orbèd space ;
Or, should she clasp thee by the morning star,
She bears thee willing captive on her jewelled car.

ABOUT THE HOMES AND HAUNTS OF BURNS.
JULY, 1894.

THE July sun in joy doth glance
   Among the Roses by the Ayr,
His day-stars o'er the Doon still dance,
   And still the ferns and flowers are fair
As when the ploughboy strung his lyre
And fanned the muse at Love's fond fire.

But who was he that o'er these streams
   Poured heavenly light transcending far
The glory of the noon-day beams
   And sweeter than the morning star ?—
A peasant poor, fell misery's heir—
The child of want and cankering care !

He read the fields I scan to-day,
   And, down the lanes of Oliphant,
His fancy with the flowers did play :—
   Ah, could I but one cadence chant
To those great eyes aye glancing still
Upon the Woodbine round the hill !

Is there a voice he heard alone
   From tuneful Nature ?   Even to me
In each flower-bell I hear some tone
   Of her soft soothing harmony :—
But I may ne'er her charms unfold
On Coila's harp of heavenly gold !

As, charm'd, some wanderer's upward gaze
   Still marks the minstrel of the sky ;
As wings the bee its bounteous ways,
   And swift can each pure fount descry—
So, captive still, the heart returns
To list the lays of Robert Burns !

IN GLEN MESSEN.

His spirit drinks mysterious awe
　　This solitude who treads
Where stern in rugged majesty
　　The mountains rear their heads.

Here could I lie on Nature's lap
　　And mark her matron smile,
And in her face divinely fair
　　Read many a truth the while.

Most fit retreat for Nature's child—
　　Far from the foils of folly—
Here read a page of Loneliness,
　　And taste sweet Melancholy.

O, list, ye souls so city sad,
　　To the solemn psalm of rills ;
Here worship to the organ-choir
　　Of the sanctuary of hills.

ADDRESS TO BARRHEAD,

*On its having, at the lang last, transformed itself into a
Burgh, and seated in the civic chair, as its first Provost,
Mr.* WILLIAM SHANKS, *2nd March, 1894.*

Nae mair my muse Parnassus spiels,
　　Tae gar my measures shine,
Sin' auld Barrhead saft tunes my reed—
　　An's voted *on the Nine !*

R

Sae, Pegasus, wi' nimble stride,
  Swift loups the Levern's banks,
Nor faulds a wing, till he maun ding
  A verse to Willie Shanks.

Ma' natal shinty-shapéd toun,
  You've touched my expectation—
You've fand, in a' your seekin' roun',
  A Prince o' Sanitation.
He's jist the very man, i' faith,
  To slush your glaury stanks ;
You need a frien' to keep you clean,
  Sae robe your Willie Shanks.

The Doctor might hae served you weel :
  He'd made a learned inspection
O' plookit weans an' chockit drains,
  An' gien you for dissection.
The Engineer, wi' head aye clear,
  Wad geared your wheels an' cranks ;
But Fortune braw has spinned her ba'—
  A goal for Willie Shanks.

Or had you throned in civic chair
  That gallant sodger, Heys—
A trustier chiel, wi' heart mair leal,
  Ne'er clam' fair Learnin's braes—
You'd pleased yoursel', and, truth I'll tell,
  You'd gained a bardie's thanks ;
But, Muse, keep time, you're at your prime ;
  Your theme is Willie Shanks.

He'll wear his chain an' honours braw
 Wi' ne'er a spark o' pride,
Unless it be " the pride o' worth "
 Whilk honest men ne'er hide.
An' what if fame shall tout his name
 As through the Wast she spanks ?
Or auld Barrhead fresh tune her reed
 In praise o' Willie Shanks ?—

He's worthy o't, an' muckle mair ;
 And hark, auld toun, tae me—
Aye use him weel, gif you wad spiel
 On firm Prosperity.
Sae here's guid health, ma' doughty knight,
 Aye foremost in the ranks ;
You've won the day, and noo we'll say—
 Not *Willie—Provost* Shanks ! *

WINSOME NELL.

Tune—" Ye banks an' braes," or another.

RESPECTFULLY DEDICATED TO THE PAISLEY TANNAHILL
CHOIR.

WHEN Nature gems her evening veil
 An' love hath tuned the Blackbird's lay ;
When shines the Primrose, luna-pale,
 And Sorrel† robes in " Dawn o' day ; "

---

* Doctor John M'Kinlay was made a Bailie. The " Engineer "—Mr. John Cochrane—was also created a Bailie. Colonel Heys succeeded Mr. Shanks as Provost.

† The wood-sorrel ; examine its beauty to understand the imagery.

Wi' love-light heart I joyous stray
    Amid Glentyan's woody dell;
There list the birds and burnie's play,
    An' meet my ain dear Winsome Nell!

O, Flora's fairest treasures hing
    Amang thy glades, Glentyan fair ;—
The angel Snawdrap hails the Spring,
    The Hyacinth perfumes the air :
But sweetest Rose may ne'er compare,
    Nor gay Laburnum's gowden spell,
Wi' her my beating bosom's care—
    My life's fond treasure—Winsome Nell!

Awa' ye cankerin' cares o' earth—
    Awa' ye dull deluded train
Wha nightly count your coffer's worth—
    Your life is but a dismal strain :
Gay Nature's charms to me are gain,
    They mak' my heart wi' rapture swell !—
Gie me the Throstle's wild refrain—
    Glentyan's woods, an' Winsome Nell !

SUNSET ON THE MONT-BLANC.

THE evening air is cool, and clear, and calm,
    I view entranced—in Majesty's array,
From a shoulder of the mighty Col de Balme,
    The Alps (the crowning prospect of the toilsome day),
In scintillating caps of ermine snow,
And glacier garments glittering blue below.

In giant pomp to kiss the evening star,
　No jealous cloud to doubt his sovereign right,
Rose Europe's mighty monarch mount afar,
　Whose awful form of dread and silent might
Beckoned the spirit from its icy throne,
To leave mankind awhile and be alone.

Silent steals evening o'er Chamounix's vale.
　Chasing the shadows to the mountain's crest;
(Silent as steals the lover's evening tale,
　Chasing all doubting from his true love's breast)
Till Blanc's soft virgin snows by Sol's soft sway,
In blushing amours greet his rapturous ray.

Now the deep worship of the soul awakes!
　Behold the mount with heavenly fire aglow,
O'er peak and dome the kindling glory shakes;
　Spreading in beauty o'er the beauteous snow,
Like Innocence on Virtue sweetly smiling,
Or pensive muse the poet's fancy wiling.

Fast fades the glory! So fades earth's fond dreams,
　All, save the soul's wrapt fancy, steals away:
Silence sits throned on high above the streams,
　And round Blanc's summit gathers evening gray,
And out heaven's blue drops many a golden star,
And the full orbed moon wheels up her silvery car.

Night is abroad in Chamounix's long vale,
　One farewell gleam illumes the monarch's head;
There is no sound the silence to assail,
　Save where the Arve sighs o'er its granite bed;
Apollo's steeds now plough the Atlantic's wave,
And shake their silvery manes above the sea-boy's grave.

TO THE SHADE OF BURNS.

25TH JANUARY, 1894.

As years roll on, in strife and din,
  Into the silent past,
Thy tide of song still floweth in
  Through Time's loud roaring blast !—
And louder still thy numbers beat
As generations onward fleet !

The casket of thy deathless soul
  In ashes lieth low ;
But while the ages onward roll
  Thy harmonies shall blow
About Humanity's great heart
A soothing solace to impart.

I see thee 'mid the Elysian shades—
  Thy brow with Daisies dight ;
Thy great eye glancing thro' the glades
  That banish erring Night,—
And clear from out that flower-crown'd throng
I hear the echoes of thy song !

Prophetic bard ! I hail the day
  That lit thy hallow'd fire ;
And joyous own the raptured sway
  Of thy immortal lyre !
And clearer still the trump of Fame
Adown the years shall sound thy name !

SONG—UNCHANGED MY LOVE ABIDETH.

My love is not a fleeting flower
　That dies beneath the blast;
Nor is it, Love, a sunny hour
　That smileth and is past.

　　　Tho' love be young and love be old,
　　　Tho' love be weak, and love be bold
　　　　And oft in triumph rideth;
　　　Tho' love be tender and be strong—
　　　And oft is short and oft is long—
　　　　Unchanged my love abideth!

In sunshine and in shadow, still
　My love to thee shall flow
For ever, like the gathering rill
　That deeper still doth grow.

　　　Tho' love doth run, he oft doth creep,
　　　And in the dark he oft doth sleep,
　　　　And his keen arrow hideth :—
　　　Till death's dark sea engulph my heart
　　　'Tis thine, my love, in every part—
　　　　Unchanged my love abideth!

HOPE.

A PAGAN bard, as auld's the rocks,
Tells hoo man's woes in blackest flocks
Flew frae Pandora's weddin' box—
　　　An' left but thee :
But surely some ane did thee coax
　　　Abroad to flee ?

Yes, Hope, I doubt that auld warld fable ;
For, och ! this earth wad be a babel,
An' mankind a' wear mantles sable—
  But thy fair form
Can half the direst darts disable
  In Life's lang storm !

I think thou wast in Eden born
On that dark, dismal, waefu' morn
Whan man was o' his glory shorn—
  By Satan speared :
Yea, frae his teeth the prey was torn
  Whan thou appeared !

Withouten thee we a' might stray,
Without a path, in dark dismay ;
But thou mak'st straught ilk crookit way
  O'er moors and fells ;
An' whan we're weary on Life's brae
  Thou diggest wells.

Thou art o' hope a maid o' micht—
Or star that shines in mirkest nicht ;
Thou'rt wi' the valiant for the richt
  Tho' sair oppress'd ;
An' in Death's dale thou art a licht
  That's aft confess'd.

Without thee Faith were whiles sair faggit ;
Wi' thee, Heaven's highest fruit she'll bag it,
An' through celestial gates she'll nag it
  Whar Reason reels ;—
Troth, far ahint has aften laggit
  Her chariot wheels !

Thou laughest in the simmer showers ;
Wi' Love thou reign'st in rosy bowers
Thou singest high on Alpine towers
   O' granite-lore ;
And gi'est mankind maist godlike powers
   To learn aye more.

Thou'rt wi' the farmer 'mong his stooks ;
Thou jinkest 'mong the student's books ;
To lovers in sweet flowery nooks
   Thou gi'est a croon,
An' aye thou shin'st wi' chubby looks
   I' the honeymoon.

Thou flashest in the poet's e'e ;
Thou starr'st the sailor ower the sea ;
Thou art the soldier's panoply
   'Mid battle's shock ;
On Science thou blink'st bonnilie—
   Fair blue-eyed Hope.

Thou'rt wi' the digger in his hole ;
Thou'rt wi' a Nansen near the Pole ;
An' roamest far, in places droll,
   Some hint to pop ;
Thou reignest in the human soul—
   Inspiring Hope.

The martyr's fires they canna char thee ;
The lion's teeth they canna scar thee ;
The dungeon's doors they canna bar thee—
   There thou shin'st bright ;
The fiends o' darkness canna mar thee,
   Thou nymph o' light.

That ravin', red-e'ed fiend, Despair,
Wi' haggard limbs an' tauted hair ;
An' her half-sister, canker'd Care—
    Guid keep us a'
Whan that ill-faur'd, inhuman pair
    Drives thee awa'.

The poet's harp shall be unstrung ;
The warrior's shield in hall be hung ;
But thou shalt reign for ever young,
    Man's heaven to ope ;
Until all human tears are wrung
    Thou'rt Angel Hope.

THE POET.

HAST thou once viewed his palace fair ?—
    O, hast thou seen the Poet's home ?—
It riseth beautcous in the air—
    Imagination is its dome !

Go, see him, fleet, fair Fancy tending
    To glorify the evening star ;
Or, through the pearly Morning wending
    To gem Aurora's crystal car !

Or wilt thou with the Poet stand
    Tip-toe on yon high throne-like cloud ?
Or canst thou hear his music grand—
    Now dulcet sweet—now thunder loud ?

Or hast thou watched him pensive stray
   When all the glories of the West
In purple robes infold the Day
   From sable Night in star-light dressed ?

Beyond the suns he tarries long
   Amid the music of the spheres ;
But thou mayest never hear the song
   Or harmonies the Poet hears !

To him belong dread Time and Space—
   Through these he walks alone serene :
His smile illumes the fair sweet face
   Of Nature—his belovèd queen.

He beareth Beauty in his eyes—
   She beameth forth o'er Nature's realm ;
Nor Chance nor Fortune him surprise,
   Nor storms of wrath his spirit whelm !

His love-lit wand doth gently lift
   From mortals their sin-heavy load ;
And in Life's lute he makes no rift—
   He singeth by the throne of God !

He singeth not as thou dost sing—
   He prayeth not as thou dost pray :
He drinketh Change's bubbling spring—
   He liveth in unending Day !

TO 1896,

WHICH CLOSED WITH RUMOURS OF WAR WITH AMERICA.

WITH pledges of good-will and social cheer,
We cannot welcome thee, thou youngling year ;
For on thy brow there broods a dark'ning cloud,
And all thy garments smell of smoke ; and loud
Amid thy train is heard the blast of War,
And thou com'st vengeful neath the blood-dyed star !
O, tell us, Ninety-Six ! canst thou declare
What waits our race on ocean, earth, in air,
In thy short span of life ?   Bid doubting cease
With one soft message from the Prince of Peace.
We thought in thee our brightest hopes to fix :
But mourn thy advent—gloomy Ninety-Six !

In Memoriam :

JAMES SHAW, *Schoolmaster, Tynron, Dumfriesshire, died
there 15th July, 1896, aged seventy years.   An ardent
admirer of Nature—a true poet and friend.*

BESIDE the murm'ring Shinell clear
　　We've laid thee down to rest ;
But its sweet sooch thou can'st not hear :
　　Nor can thy loving breast
With rapture swell at sight of Rose
　　Or rainbowed butterfly :—
Thy ashes rest in long repose—
　　Thy spirit wings on high !

O, thou did'st love all beauteous things—
　Could'st read fair Nature's page
With poet's eye, by rippling springs,
　Or where loud torrents rage
Down mountain scars.　And every flower
　For thee had message sweet ;
And bird and beast in field and bower
　Were thy companions meet !

Gone !　Best and wisest I have known—
　Earth gives me not another ;
A pall o'er Nature's face is thrown,
　Since thou hast passed, by brother !—　＼ my
Hope says—Beyond Death's doleful dale,
　Where fairest flowers fade never,
With joy we may each other hail,
　Along the crystal river.

A HOLIDAY AT THE HOMES AND HAUNTS
OF SHAKESPERE.

AT WARWICK CASTLE.

Not with the breathing canvas, charmed with age,
Adorning halls ancestral, are my thoughts ;
Nor on those priceless treasures of fair art
From many lands—but with a host unseen,
The ghosts of warriors that, bright mailed, once
　　thronged
This stately pile : and vows of hate or love
From manly times like wandering echoes come :
And Sadness in this place hath set her throne !

AT ANNE HATHAWAY'S COTTAGE.

"Anne hath a way"—oft would he say
Who rules the realm of Song ;
And, truth to say, she had a way
That never led him wrong !

IN SHAKESPERE'S BIRTH-PLACE.

(Shakespere)
Of Poesy the flower and fruit—
Imagination's rarest blossom,
Born to be King of all who sing—
His throne, for aye the human bosom.

AT KENILWORTH CASTLE.

Still chased by Love's sharp arrows keen
Here Amy stole, like hunted deer ;
Here poured her sorrows to a queen
That rarely dropped Compassion's tear.

Cold are the hearts that here beat warm :
The bosoms stilled that warred Love's waves :
Here Pageantry no more can charm—
Where Ruin rules a realm of Graves.

ODE TO BURNS, FOR THE CENTENARY OF HIS DEATH, 1896.

A CENTURY hath flown,
Since, weak and wan and lone,
The Lily of the Lyre in dust was laid :

But still its odour sweet
Scenteth the years that fleet—
Wafteth through Life's alarms, sunshine and shade ;
Nor can such redolence depart—
But sweetly soothing blows about the human heart !

When, by the Nith's clear wave,
The MORTAL found a grave.
Th' IMMORTAL on Fame's chariot heavenward flew,
Winged with the name of Burns
(That Dissolution spurns)
And round the World her silver Trump she blew,
Which wider, clearer, through the years,
Humanity's great heart with growing rapture hears !

Burns, with celestial fire,
Did swift transmute the Lyre
From rusting brass to strings of trembling gold ;
And by the Doon and Ayr
Uttered such Music rare,
That Earth, enthralled, bowed to the Minstrel bold :—
He dewed with Song the daisied lea,
And o'er his native vales showered heavenly harmony !

With sympathetic song
He charmed the common throng,
And lowly things did raise to heights of glory :—
With seer's keen eye did trace
In every brother's face
Some record of Life's blurred and blotted story :—
With Prophet's gaze beheld the day
When Love o'er all the Earth shall bear its sovereign
sway.

His is the Fire to smite
Old Wrong that rides on Might !
He bids the steeds of Tyranny unyoke :
And of the Brave and Good
Mouldeth one Brotherhood
That makes Oppression's Throne to reel and rock :
Though Nature's face he sweet doth scan,
His Lyre's bold numbers roll in sympathy with Man.

As trills the Lark on high—
Circling the azure sky,
Witching our ears with rich angelic strains :
So Burns, the Lyre's crowned King,
Doth ever, soaring, sing,
Leading our willing hearts with golden reins :—
The Centuries shall never mar
His upward Choral flight toward the Morning Star !

BURNS ANNIVERSARY, 1891.

'TWAS a howling night, and the snow fell fast,
As I mused by the ingle's glare,
When a maid stepped in from the angry blast,
And her form was fearfully fair.
'Twas Fancy : the Queen of the Poet's light
And the soul of his quenchless fire ;
And she said—" I must crown the bard to-night
In the midst of the ninefold choir.
I will wing me back to my summer bowers
And the glens where the burnie shimmers,
Where the cascade sings in its silvery showers
And the flame of the May-flower glimmers.

I will gather the woodbine, bean, and rose,
    And the ivy's fadeless green,
And each fairest flower in the field that blows,
    Or that kisses the river's sheen ;
And I'll twine them sweet in a crown of light
    To the car of immortal fame,
With daisies diamonded and dight,
    And the holly's winter flame :
And I'll wheel aloft where the ninefold choir
    And the great immortals throng—
Where the bard of mankind strikes his lyre
    In the halls of deathless song :
And I'll crown him on this, his natal day,
    With a wreath that never dies
While the power and passion of his lay
    In the human bosom rise ! "

ODE

To commemorate the Jubilee of Messrs. Zechariah Heys & Sons, South Arthurlie Print Works, Barrhead. Written by Mr. James Rigg, a former employé, and recited by Mr. Alex. M'Phail Stewart at the Banquet given by the firm in the Golden Lion Hotel, Stirling, on Saturday, the 18th June, 1892—Chairman, Colonel Zechariah John Heys of Stonehouse, Barrhead ; Croupiers, Lieutenant-Colonel Zechariah Henry Heys of Rockmount, Barrhead, and Zechariah George Heys, Esq., of Springhill, Barrhead. About ninety sat down to dinner.

Now fifty summer suns have shone,
    And fifty weary winters fled,
Six hundred silvery moons have gone,
    Since first there rose above Barrhead
A star that still doth brightly blaze,
And bears the charméd name of Heys.

From Lennox fells six pioneers,
  The grand old sire, five noble sons,
All full of hope and void of fears,
  Pitched fast their tent where Levern runs :
The book of years tells what they've done ;
But of the brave there's left but one.

Methinks I see the primal chief,
  His kindly gait, his dauntless eye ;
With word so tender, yet so brief—
  The inward sight to quick descry.
A type of all true men and ways
Was staunch old Zechariah Heys.

And still the name is ever green
  In city, town, and busy mart ;
In generations three we've seen
  Heredity still play its part,
For manly youth doth still aspire
To tread the path of such a sire.

To-day, from Stirling's ancient rock
  We view the fields where heroes fell,
And fearless met grim battle's shock—
  Whose dauntless fame the muses tell ;
But Art may now her peans raise
And sing the Jubilee of Heys.

Can my poor muse the deeds proclaim
  Of fifty years of nobler strife,
Or celebrate the well-won fame
  Of men who've lived an honoured life ?
'Twould need a Burns to bind the bays
Around the lustrous name of Heys.

When our good ship first shook her sides,
  Of larger guns* she had but three ;
But mark how proudly now she rides
  In splendour in Port Jubilee !
For, tho' through Flood and Fire oft driven,
*She thunders now her Twenty-seven.**

Alas ! what memories throng the mind
  While treading through the chequered past !
We hear sad moaning in the wind,
  See pale Death riding on the blast ;
With lamentations, sobs, and tears,
Sad prelude to these fifty years.†

Where are the faces once we knew—
  The merry laugh, the friendly tear ?
All quickly fading from our view,
  And faint and far their voice we hear.
Let's think o' them where'er they be,
In this glad year of Jubilee.

But you, my merry mates to-day,
  Let's pledge success—let cheers be given :
Let Stirling's rock itself be gay,
  All sadness to the shades be driven,
And let it be the queen of days
That blows the Jubilee of Heys.

Now let us sing " Long live our Queen,"
  And " Longer live South Arthurlie ; "
Rich golden harvests may it glean,
  And foster fair Prosperity,
Until its years in number be
Like stars upon a sleeping sea.

---

* Printing Machines.   † Referring to the appalling catastrophe,
the bursting of Glanderstone Dam.

In Memoriam:

Mr. WALTER MacLELLAN, *died at Blairvaddick, Row, Gareloch, 17th June, 1889.*

O'ER Gare's sweet rippling waters darkness rests,
The sunshine of a face that cheer'd its shore
Hath sunk in night. From us for evermore
The smile benignant—that in all our breasts
Told of a heart infraught with pure bequests—
Hath pass'd away. The countenance that spoke
Of inward calm, and in true men awoke
A thousand charities as welcome guests,
Is pall'd by death !

                        The mart he did adorn ;
And added grace to all its rugged ways,
And Labour was the sweetness of his days.
The city he might pace with Honour's mien.
Faith found him waiting for the heavenly morn,
And earth for long shall keep his memory green.

ANDREW FERRIER SHANKS, *died 12th May, 1893.*

WELL done, brave knight, in Christ's sure armour clad !
    Thou, ever foremost in the ranks of peace,
That, with the sun, each day did make *one* glad ; *
    The King hath given thee rest and bless'd release.

---

* The deceased gentleman, for many years prior to his death, made it a part of his daily duty to make at least one person happy. What a blessed valley the Levern would traverse if this were more practised by rich and poor !

And we that, weeping, watched thy welkin flight,
  Scarce caught the hidden harmonies that hung
About a life that strove for Truth and Right;
  Nor missed the harp till Death its chords unstrung.

Thy voice, that ever spake to edify,
  Is hushed for ever 'neath the flowery sod;
Thy soul, whose pinions ever soared on high,
  Now folds its wings within the *rest* of God.

Yes, thou art gone!   But yet the memory
  Of all thy kindly ways, like clusters sweet
Of white Radanthus blossoms, still shall be
  Hung round our hearts and homes while Time doth
    fleet.

SONNET TO J. LINDSAY, AN AGED LITERARY FRIEND.

THOU that did'st ope to me the golden gates
Of Wisdom, and did'st lead my longing soul
Through Poesy's sweet meads, where Fancy waits
To touch the lips with song—let me extol
Thy cherished favours.   Could my numbers roll
Full as the tide of Memory that elates
My being, and the Wisdom contemplates
Of thy weighed words—now written on Time's scroll—
My song should bear the image and the grace
That round thy sober speech do ever play,
Or else the Lore deep chisell'd in thy face
That speaks a mind where all that's pure holds sway:
For, he who scans like thee dread Time and Space,
Lives, loves, and longs in one unclouded day!

LINES ON THE CLOSE OF 1893.

(The year was noted for its advanced Spring and early Harvest.)

ANOTHER year in judgment sits
   On us, the erring sons of men !
Alas ! how Time, in silence, flits
   Across our "Threescore years and ten " !—
Did Caution mark his fitful face,
Old Wisdom by his side might pace !

Yes ! Thou art gone, old Ninety-three !—
   (Perhaps, to Fancy, thou art dead,)—
And thou wert sure full fair to see !—
   What golden harvests thou did'st spread !
How quickly Spring fair Flora woo'd—
How soon ripe Autumn's face we viewed !

For Friendship, fresh as fragrant flowers,—
   For Love that reigneth ever young—
For social joys and hallowed hours—
   Ev'n for the griefs that hearts have wrung—
A grateful Faith looks back to thee,
Thou sent-of-God, old Ninety-three !

Young Ninety-four ! we hail with hope
   Thy coming ! May our youngest year
To fairy Science vistas ope :
   May waiting Earth some waftings hear
Of that full swelling Harmonie
When Christ shall of his Travail see !

THE PEESWEEP INN.

Tune—" Soldier's Joy."

The following verses may help to keep in remembrance the delightful excursions made for many a year by " the Squad"—the endearing
name of the committee of the Barrhead Mechanics' Institute, the first
Mechanics' Institute ever formed in Scotland, I believe. I have no
doubt, however, but the verses will find an echo in the breasts of the
Ramblers and kindred associations in and around Glasgow and Paisley,
who were wont, once a year, to make a pilgrimage o'er the Gleniffer
Braes to the above world-famed muirland hostelry, over which our
Justices have thrown a pall.

WHEN the last o' bielded snaw
Frae Ben Lomond skips awa',
An' the floods, deep roarin', fa'
    Ower the Craigie Linn ;
Then come the flowery days
When we hie us o'er the braes—
Jist to hear what Nature says
    At the Peesweep Inn !

O, the Daisy's on the sod,
An' the Squad are on the road,
Through the mairs they aft hae trod
    'Mang the gowden Whin ;
An' the Lark is singing high
Whaur the Snipe and Plover cry—
An' wi' joyous hearts we hie
    To the Peesweep Inn !

Here's the Peesweep on the sign.
First a drap o' Hielan' wine,
That ilk man his care may tine—
    Let the sports begin !

See, L-t-r's on the stump,
An' wi' laughin' gars us jump,
Till on peaty knowes we dump
    Roun' the Peesweep Inn.

Then, in dancin' circled quorum,
M-rr-y gies us "Tullochgorum "—
Worth hauf a hunner score um
    That in ha's mak' a din ;
While Br--m, sae "neat and handy,"
Gies us "Yankee Doodle Dandy,"
'Mang the trees sae bow'd and bandy,
    Roun' the Peesweep Inn.

But, hungry noo as clegs,
We sit doon to ham an' eggs,
An' the seer a blessin' begs
    Frae the Pow'rs aboon ;
While, wi' cakes an' soda scones,
Od, the rustic table groans,
An' the tea flees oot like rhones
    At the Peesweep Inn.

Syne, roun' the reekin' bowl,
Sang an' sentiment maun roll,
Whilk great L-nd-y maun control,
    For we mak' sic a din ;
Yet, like brithers a', we twine
Roun' the days o' auld langsyne—
Sic a sicht might draw the *Nine*
    To the Peesweep Inn !

Wi' monie a loud encore,
An' monie a random splore,
O' fun we had galore
    Till the rise o' the moon—

Till night cam' on apace
An' shot in his bruckie face :—
Syne we left that classic place
    Ca'd the " Peesweep Inn " !

.   .   .   .   .   .

Nae mair we'll climb the brae
On a bonnie simmer day,
An' join sic merry fray,
    Flingin' care to the win';—
There's a moanin' on the road,
Sin' the fiat's gaen abroad,
An' there's written " *Ikabod* "
    O'er the Peesweep Inn !

In Memoriam :

The REV. DR. OLIVER FLETT, *died suddenly at Sannox,
Arran, 20th August, 1894, aged 64 years.*

AMID the glories of the Alpine isle,
    Thy soul, sure pinioned, took its homeward flight,
Meek shepherd, in whose steps we marked no guile,
    Thy bleating flock is cloaked in tearful night.

No more to sylvan pastures shall thy crook
    Lead gently by the streams of Zion fair ;
No more thy glance illume the holy Book—
    Thy voice no more lead heavenward in prayer.

Gone ! faithful one ! yet sweet is now thy rest,
    Where earth's wan, weary woes can ne'er assail ;
Thou art at peace upon thy Father's breast,
    And we, awhile, must tread this tearful vale.

In Memoriam:

PETER DENNY, Esq., LL.D., Dumbarton, *died 22nd August, 1895, aged 74 years.*

WHEN conquerors bend to grim unconquered Death,
  And leave their empires and their glories, won
By sword and cannon : then, with trumpet breath,
  Fame rings their battles while the ages run !
Yet goodness walketh not through war-clouds' dun,
  And deathless deeds rise not from heaps of slain !—
The truly noble earthly plaudits shun ;
  Their bliss to find a balm for human pain :—
  These tune the poet's lyre to many a soothing strain !

Of such was he whom Clutha's sons now weep !
  His triumphs ride o'er every ocean's wave !
Where'er fair Commerce round the world doth sweep
  To bless mankind and free the shackled slave,
She beareth back immortelles for the grave
  Of him whose heart o'erflowed with pity still,
Whose love did oft the brow of Sorrow lave,
  Whose bounty large old Want did ever fill,
  Whose tongue aye spake to bless, whose mouth ne'er
    uttered ill !

We've laid his dust in Nature's tender lap !
  Our sea-king's spirit is in haven " Fair,"
The form beloved with daisied sod we hap,
  And with his kin unfeigned sorrow share !
Would that, like him, our barque we might prepare
  For " Homeward Bound," 'neath Faith's all-powerful
    sail,
That catcheth full the sweet celestial air,
  That rides us safe, through many a bitter gale,
  On to the golden shore—beyond earth's woe and wail!

TO THE ALPS.

(Written in the Vale of Chamounix.)

THE Alps ! the Alps !   The snow-capp'd Alps,
   The poet's contemplation ;
Whose awful forms, that dare the storms,
   Seem the king-works of Creation !

The Alps ! the Alps ! the glorious Alps—
   The palaces of wonder ;
Where the tall pine waves, and the torrent raves,
   And the avalanche leaps in thunder !

O, the bracing air from your glaciers bare,
   'Neath your mighty thrones of glory—
Where'er I be, seem part of me—
   A song in Life's short story !

HELEN.

THY een are like twin Brambles black,
   Glittering 'mong the dew ;
And the hiniest pear, at the fa' o' the year,
   Ne'er matched thy luscious mou !

TO A THRUSH I HEARD SING IN THE AFTERNOON OF THE SHORTEST DAY.

SAY, thou that makest poets dream,
By flowery glade and purling stream,
What gave thee that untimely theme ?
   Think'st thou 'tis Spring ?

That twig, erewhile a scented spray,
Hath not a leaf, nor green nor grey,
And yet on this, the shortest day,
  What makes thee sing ?

Dost thou not mark bleak Boreas stand,
To lead his crispy-arrowed band,
To lay beneath his icy hand,
  Wood, lake, and bower ?

And thou dost pour thy mellow song
Beneath grim Winter's batteries strong,
While youth, and age, and beauty throng
  Thy Poplar tower.

Perhaps the love that lurks in dells,
That tinkles in the sweet blue-bells,
Inflates thy bosom with strange spells
  That burst in song.

Dost thou this day, so short and drear,
Feel pulsings of the unborn year,
Like hope, that comes my heart to cheer,
  When vexed with wrong ?

Or through thy being doth there stray
The image of an April day,
With shimmering birks and willows gay
  Above thy head ?

Whate'er it be, my thanks, sweet thrush !
Ah ! blinding snows thy hymn shall hush,
Or Death thy hopes and mine shall crush
  Amongst the dead.

GRACE.

(Written in the album of a young lady, whose Christian name was Grace).

Could I, with Ruben's magic brush,
    One perfect form on canvas trace ;
I'd make all meaner plaudits hush,
    And all men own " Yes ! that is Grace."

Or could I, like a Phidias, turn,
    From marble white, the fairest face ;
With admiration men should burn—
    And each exclaim—" Yes ! that is Grace."

Or could I, with a Shakespeare's eyes,
    Through Fancy's realm for ever pace ;
I'd meet no rarer, sweeter prize
    Than just the witching form of " *Grace.*"

Envoi.

When I, ere long, Time's service leave,
    The King hath promised me a place ;
In this I've had no hand, I grieve,
    O, no ! It's all been done by " *Grace.*"

In Memoriam:

H. R. H. The Duke of Clarence and Avondale.

(Born 8th January, 1864; Died 14th January, 1892.)

For which the Princess graciously thanked the author.

O DEATH, dark lurker round our brightest days !
  Can famished millions or grim battle's gore
Not glut thy rav'ning maw ? Thy hidden ways
  Lead to the gates of bliss !—one triumph more !
And England bows to thee—deep smitten sore.
  Young Hope, high prowed, on Time's uncertain tide
For Hymen's happy haven proudly bore ;
  And Love—flower crowned—sang o'er the waters
    wide :
  But thy fierce blast, O Death ! hath wrecked an
    Empire's pride.

Rest, Clarence ! Hope of England, calmly sleep !
  No war cloud o'er thy bier doth darkly frown !
Above thee shall the Snowdrop yearly weep—
 . The sword of Truth hath won thee thy renown,
  And we 'mong flowers white have laid thee down !
High gleamed in thy young eye Earth's loftiest throne :
  Thine eye is dimmed ! But thou hast gained a crown
With glory gemmed : then why should hearts be lone ?
Since Faith's quick upward glance may follow where
    thou'rt gone !

To H. R. H. The Princess of Wales.